SOPHIE AND SCOTTIE'S

Adventures of
Something's Fishy

To: Emma

Keep discovering!

Cindy C. Murray

Cindy C. Murray

Sophie and Scottie's Adventures
of Something's Fishy

Copyright © 2015 Cindy C. Murray

Published by 📖Madmac Press

For publishing and distribution inquires contact:
Madmac Press
858-337-1102
Rowlett, TX 75088

Printed in the United States of America

ISBN-13: 978-1732313415

Library of Congress Control Number 2015933215

Cover art by Molly Alice Hoy
Book design by Drew Bailey

Dedicated with love to my brother, Scotty.

Table
of
Contents

CHAPTER ONE

Molly and a Creepy Crawly

Sophie and Scottie's room looked the same after they returned from their amazing Mexico adventure. As they walked back through the magical frame, Scottie looked behind her and the frame instantly shrunk back to its original size, perfect for when Auntie Jill sends them another photograph.

"Let's go find Ma and Pa," Sophie almost shouted. "It seems like we haven't seen them in a long time!"

The sisters dropped their backpacks and headed for the large living room, almost running as they turned the corner of the hallway. As they entered the room, they saw Ma and Pa talking to a man in a chair with his back to them.

"Oh, here are my girls, and in such a hurry I see," Ma said in amusement as they ran up to hug her.

"We have a guest," Pa said as the man stood up to turn toward them.

Both girls gasped, instantly looked at each other, and then looked at the man.

"This is Dr. Rusty Drake," Pa introduced to them. "Dr. Drake, these are our two daughters, Sophie and Scottie."

The girls walked toward him in shock as he took their hands and shook them.

"It's so nice to meet you two. I've heard a lot about you from your Aunt Jill," he said with a wink. "Oh, and by the way," Dr. Drake continued with a smile, "I have an envelope from your aunt to give you."

Sophie and Scottie, still stunned, didn't move.

"Well, is anyone going to take the envelope from Dr. Drake?" Pa asked while standing with one hand in his front jeans pocket.

Both girls reached for the envelope he was holding. Dr. Drake looked the same as when the girls said goodbye to him in Mexico. He had those smiling blue eyes, a thick and scraggly looking dark brown beard, and a straight pointy nose. He was a little taller than Pa, with a big barrel of a chest.

"I think it's a photograph!" Sophie exclaimed breathlessly to Scottie.

Scottie took the envelope from Dr. Drake, opened it, and peeked inside. She looked up at the man and then to Sophie and said excitedly, "I think you're right!"

Scottie quickly closed the envelope, knowing that she and Sophie weren't ready to look at the picture yet. Both girls were still amazed and tired from the last adventure the magical frame had given them. Sophie understood why Scottie didn't want to show Ma and Pa the photo.

"Well, let's see the picture that Auntie Jill sent you girls," Ma ordered.

"Oh, we'll show it to you later," Sophie blurted out. "We need to go check on Fuzzy Mama and her baby lamb in the barn before the sun sets."

"I thought you just did that," Pa commented.

"We did," Scottie answered quickly. "But after we saw Fuzzy, we also checked on Starburst and Firefly. You know how those horses want their late-day sugar cube and a neck rub while we brush their long manes."

"Yes, and then we raced up here from the stables," Sophie interrupted. "So we'll put this envelope in our bedroom and then go check on that cute baby and Fuzzy Mama one more time," Sophie said with a smile while looking at Scottie.

"It was nice meeting you, Dr. Drake," both girls said at the same time, as twins often do.

(The twins were not identical, but each girl had the same small nose and shaped mouth and chin. Sophie's eyes were green, and she had long straight dark-brown hair with red highlights. In contrast, Scottie's eyes were blue, and she had long wavy red hair with blond streaks through it, often saying it was the kiss of the sun that made her hair have such beautiful blonde highlights.)

"Why, it was nice meeting you two as well," Dr. Drake replied with a smile and a twinkle in his eye. "I hope I'll see you girls again soon."

Sophie and Scottie gave him a quick hug and ran out of the living room and back to their bedroom. They could hear Dr. Drake give a deep laugh as they approached the hallway. Once the girls reached their room, Sophie peaked out into the hall before she carefully closed their door.

"Whew, that was close!" Scottie exclaimed, still holding the envelope that Auntie Jill had sent them.

"I know," Sophie agreed. "I can't believe Dr. Drake is here in our house. How did he get to the house so fast from the Crystal Canyon?" Sophie thought out loud.

"I'm not sure. Maybe Dr. Drake has his own magical frame too," Scottie answered thoughtfully as she put the envelope down on their oak table.

Both girls looked at the magical frame that Auntie Jill had given them. It still looked the same as it did before their adventure to Mexico, with hundreds of tiny mirrored crystals covering it and a large diamond-shaped crystal in the middle of the top of the frame.

"The frame seems so normal," Scottie commented as she looked at it displayed on their round oak table in the "safe" zone of their bedroom. "It isn't glowing or changing colors or getting larger. No, it just looks normal."

Just as Scottie said that, the frame suddenly slid across the table next to the envelope! It seemed to come alive with colors of soft yellow, then bright yellow, then soft orange, and then bright orange. In fact, it was as if the frame was breathing yellow and orange. Suddenly, as if with a sigh, the frame went from bright blue to sky blue and back to its beautiful clear and silver crystals.

"Oh, boy," Sophie said, "this is the frame we know! I think we are going to have to keep the envelope separate from the frame. How about we give it to Ma for safe-keeping, even though I'm not sure how we are going to explain to Ma why we don't want to keep it in our room."

"I know what to say. Just leave it to me," Scottie said with a smile.

"Okay, but first we should go check on Fuzzy Mama and her adorable baby," Sophie agreed.

As the girls were about to leave the room, Scottie quickly turned back to the table to pick up the envelope.

"We don't want to leave this here when we're not in the room. You never know what might happen to the frame with the picture so close to it," Scottie said with assurance.

"Good thinking, sis," Sophie said and she and Scottie walked out of their room toward the front door of the house.

As the girls skipped down to the barn, they heard a barking noise just outside the barn door.

"Look, Sophie. It's Molly! I wonder what she's barking at and what is she doing here?"

"Doesn't she belong to Mr. Wilson?" Sophie asked Scottie, referring to their postal worker.

"Yes, she does," Jack, Pa's ranch help, said as he came walking from the side of the barn. "Mr. Wilson asked if we wanted her because he can't keep Molly anymore. He says that he's gone too much and knows that you girls would take great care of her."

"That's awesome," the girls shouted at the same time.

They bent down on their knees to scratch Molly's thick fur. She was a husky and shepherd mix of some kind with piercing blue eyes. Her pointy black ears were perked up and ready to play. In fact, most of her fur was black except for her white chest, white paws, and a white dot on each side of her hips. Just the tip of her tail was in a little curl. Molly was very playful, with lots of tail wagging and endless kisses!

"Okay, let's go check on Fuzzy Mama and give her new straw. Then we can play with Molly some more. She's a young dog—I think she's only three years old—and so full of energy," Scottie said with a laugh.

Scottie then stood up and slid open the barn, making sure that Molly didn't get in and scare the baby lamb.

"Here, Scottie, give me the envelope and I'll set it over here on this shelf. We don't want to bend it before we give it to Ma for safekeeping."

"Okay, but let's not forget to get it before we leave the barn," Scottie said and gave the envelope to Sophie.

Just inside the barn door was a 10-foot dusty workbench with tools and jars full of nails and bolts. Above and along the length of the workbench were several shelves. The lowest shelf on the end of the bench is where Sophie could reach, and that is where she put the envelope before she and Scottie cleaned Fuzzy's birthing pen.

Each girl felt as if she hadn't seen Fuzzy and the baby in days. Their adventure had taken them so far away for several days (in magical frame time), and it was nice to be back at home and back to their regular chores.

"Oh, look how sweet the baby is with his fluffy black face! He's nuzzling up to Fuzzy and beginning to suckle," Sophie observed as they began to clean the birthing pen.

The girls put the soiled straw in a wheelbarrow for Jack to take to the giant waste bin for burning. The ranch took care of all of its own animal-related waste, recycling and composting as much as possible.

"I think we're done!" Scottie announced as she put her rake away next to the pen. "I'll get the envelope and we can give it to Ma."

"Okay," Sophie agreed while putting her rake away too. "I sure am glad that Pa put us in charge of Fuzzy Mama and the baby. I love taking care of them. They have enough water and food pellets, so let's go."

"Scottie!" Sophie suddenly shouted as she was walking up to her. "Don't move and look at me."

"Why?" Scottie asked, about to move her hand to grab the envelope.

"Just do as I say and lower your hand and walk backward!" Sophie ordered with authority.

"Okay, okay, what is…," and then Scottie quit talking and just stared at the envelope on the shelf.

There next to the envelope with one leg on it sat a very large and hairy black tarantula spider! It was black as night and partially in the shadow so it was really hard to see.

"Wow!" Sophie gasped as she carefully slid the envelope off of the shelf. "Look at how big that thing is. It's ugly and really neat at the same time. I wonder if this is what Molly was barking at."

"You are crazy. That spider is disgusting!" Scottie

15

replied as if eating something that was sour. "We'd better try to kill it."

"Oh, no you don't," Sophie said in a protective way as she walked up closer to the spider on the shelf and set the envelope down on the nearby bench. "Just look at its shiny black hairy legs with its sections. It's almost beautiful in a creepy kind of way. I know. We'll put it in one of those empty jars and release it away from the barn in the bushes."

"What do you mean, *we?*" Scottie asked, slowly shaking her head back and forth.

"We, I mean, I will save it. This kind of spider is big, but it won't harm humans. Don't you remember the school tarantula in the science classroom?"

"Now that it's summer, I choose not to remember the gross part of school," Scottie replied.

"Reach over there on the bench and hand me one of those empty jars," Sophie requested of Scottie. "No, not that one, the larger one. It looks like this spider will be six or seven inches long when it starts to walk."

"Are you sure you want to do this? Maybe we should ask Jack or Pa to 'save' your spider for you," Scottie suggested in a rather sarcastic tone.

"No, I can do this," Sophie said as if convincing herself. "I'll put the jar down in front of it and you can use the envelope to tap the spider a little so it will stand up and walk."

"You want ME to tap it?" Scottie replied, hardly believing what Sophie wanted her to do.

"Okay, I'll tap the spider with..." Sophie looked around and found a hammer with a long handle. "I'll use the head of this hammer."

Just as Sophie was about to tap the spider, it must've sensed something because in a blink of an eye, it shot forward and landed on Sophie's shoulder. She immediately leaned forward, squealing and then shaking her body like a wet dog!

This action scared Scottie so much that she screamed and jumped out of the way and then jumped up high, at least 20 feet high, almost tapping the barn's roof with her head!

With so many things going on, Sophie barely noticed Scottie. The tarantula quickly fell to the ground and, like a cockroach, was scurrying out the tiny opening next to the barn door.

"Oh, my gosh!" Scottie proclaimed. "Are you okay, Sophie?"

"Yes, yes, I'm fine," Sophie answered, brushing herself off with her hands as if she were covered in dirt. "Did I just see out of the corner of my eye what I thought I saw?"

"Well, it happened so fast, but yes, I guess I can still jump really high from our Mexico adventure," Scottie replied. With that comment, she looked at her legs and lifted up each one to make sure they still worked.

"I haven't really thought about whether we'd still have our special talents back at home," Sophie thought out loud. "See if you can do that again. Jump as high as you can."

So Scottie squatted down as if to jump over something and sprang up as fast as she could. She jumped maybe three feet.

"I guess that answers that," Scottie said disappointedly.

"Maybe it only works at home if there is an emergency or something," Sophie suggested.

"Maybe. Grab the envelope and let's head back to the house. I'm really tired," Scottie said as she slid open the barn door and Sophie followed.

"Since we're done with our chores, let's ask Pa about Molly before we go to our room," Sophie said. "With it being such a nice summer evening, I'm sure he and Ma are sitting in their favorite outdoor 'loveseat' next to the fountain. Pa is probably smoking his pipe in the courtyard while talking with Ma."

Just as she said that, Molly came running up to greet them, tail wagging and ready to play.

"Where were you a few minutes ago?" Scottie teased. "We could've used you to bark at that yucky black spider and chase it away."

"Tarantula," Sophie corrected. "We'll have to tell Ma and Pa about our little encounter with it."

"And give Ma the envelope," Scottie added.

Sophie, Scottie, and their new dog Molly ran up to the main house together. Scottie started to yell for Ma and Pa to find out where they were in the house.

"We're in the courtyard," was the reply. "I see you've met Molly," Pa said, holding his pipe and sitting next to Ma on their special loveseat.

"Just one minute," Ma interrupted, "no yelling in this house, and no dirty dogs either."

"Isn't she beautiful?" the girls stated more than questioned.

"She does have the cutest little white tip at the end of her curled black tail," Ma observed.

"We were so surprised when we heard a barking noise coming from outside the barn and then Jack told us that Molly was now our dog!" Scottie said excitedly.

"What was she barking at?" Pa asked with a grin.

"Well, we think it was this big and huge black disgusting spider!" Scottie answered with a sour look on her face.

"It was actually a picture perfect tarantula," Sophie corrected.

"Yeah, until it landed on your shoulder!" Scottie interrupted with a creepy laugh.

"It landed where?" Ma asked louder than usual.

"Oh, it kind of jumped off the shelf as we were looking at it in the barn," Sophie said, patting Ma on the shoulder to calm her a little. "It happened so fast that I really couldn't get out of its way. Once it was on the ground, the spider scurried out of the barn and into the bushes."

"And what did you do, Scottie?" Pa asked.

"Oh, I just jumped back a little to get out of the way," Scottie replied while looking at Sophie.

"Anyway, we love Molly already," Sophie changed the subject. "Where will she sleep and eat?"

"Mr. Wilson said that Molly is housebroken, so she can sleep in the screened-in porch next to the kitchen. He gave us her dog bed and an extra bag of dog food. It will be up to you girls to feed her once a day, brush her as needed, and have lots of fun with her," Ma said with a smile.

"Oh, we will do everything you said, especially the 'have fun' part," said Scottie as she bent down to pet

Molly behind her ears.

"I also think it will be a good idea for Molly to go with you on all of your trail rides on the ranch. Our 10,000-acre sheep ranch makes a large area, and I feel better with Molly being with you when you take the horses out," Pa said as he looked at what Sophie was holding.

"Is that the envelope that Dr. Drake gave you?" Pa asked

"Why, yes it is," Sophie answered before Scottie could.

"Yes, and we want to give it to you for safekeeping, Ma," Scottie added. "You see, Sophie and I are playing this sort of game we are calling..."

"The patient game," Sophie chimed in. "I don't think Scottie could last a day without looking at what Auntie Jill put in the envelope."

"And I say she can't last, so we've decided to give it to you until we end the game," Scottie stated with a smile as she took the envelope from Sophie and handed it over to Ma.

"Well, this is kind of a strange game, but I guess I'll play along," Ma said as she took the envelope. "Do you girls want to know where I will put it in the house?"

"NO!" both blurted out.

"Not knowing where you put it adds to the game," Scottie said, noticing the puzzled look on Ma's face.

"Oh, okay," Ma agreed and then went into the house to hide the envelope.

"You girls play some strange games," Pa said as he took a puff on his pipe. "Look at all of those stars in the sky."

"There's so many of them," Sophie observed as she nestled next to Pa.

Scottie let out a huge yawn and also sat next to Pa. This was one of the best times of the day when everyone could just relax in the courtyard and hear the crickets chirping after sunset.

"I sure am tired," Scottie said while yawning again. "Let's put Molly away and then go to bed."

Sophie agreed and both girls gave Pa a hug and kiss goodnight and headed to the kitchen to say goodnight to Ma after putting Molly to bed. As Sophie and Scottie entered their bedroom, they didn't notice the backpacks that Dr. Drake had given them after they had walked through the magical frame. They used them the entire time they were on their adventure in Mexico, forgetting that they were still on their backs when they walked through the frame to get back to their bedroom. Somehow, the backpacks got pushed under the five-foot-round oak table in their room. They were just so glad to be back in their own beds that they didn't really think about them or anything else.

CHAPTER TWO

Puppy Love

The girls awoke to the sounds of the rooster crowing and the smell of coffee that Ma made every morning for her and Pa. Still yawning, Scottie sat up in her bed and looked around the room. Her desk was at the foot of her bed and looked rather empty. She hadn't really used it since school got out for the summer. Scottie loved not having to hurry in the morning to get ready for school. (She always stayed in bed while Sophie used the bathroom, making her almost late for the school bus in the morning!) Yes, this was the life, no schedules and no...

"Scottie, come on, get out of bed. We have our chores to do before breakfast and I'm hungry, so let's go!" Sophie ordered from her closet.

"Oh, well, so much for no schedules," Scottie thought as she got dressed.

While Sophie waited for her, she sat on the floor to put on her cowboy boots. As she pulled them on, she noticed the backpacks under their table. She caught her breath and immediately remembered standing there in the hotel meeting Dr. Drake. He suggested she and Scottie look down to find two backpacks, which seemed to appear at their feet! This all happened after they had walked through the magical and wonderful crystal frame they'd received as a gift from Auntie Jill.

"Scottie, look! We forgot about the backpacks," Sophie announced and crawled under the table to pull them out. She put her backpack on her desk and did the same for Scottie's backpack. "I wonder if the map is still in there! I don't remember taking it out."

Sophie quickly unzipped her pack and looked inside. At the bottom of the pack under the dirty clothes from their hike in Mexico was her beautiful beaded rain box. This special box was also a gift from Auntie Jill that the girls had received before the magical frame. The special sound that came out when the lid was taken off helped to release the millions of butterflies hanging on the chains in the giant cave where they were held captive by the evil Professor Zooger. Next to the box was a rolled-up piece of paper, barely fitting into the backpack when it was zipped. Sophie almost held her breath as she pulled out both items.

"This is awesome!" Sophie exclaimed as she unrolled the large piece of paper.

"What's so awesome?" Scottie asked as she pulled her boots out of her closet.

"I think this is Maptrixter!" Sophie said as she studied the paper.

"You mean the Maptrixter that we got from Dr. Drake? Or, should I say that Trixter chose you to be its owner," Scottie remembered.

"Yes, this is it, and now the map is of our ranch," Sophie said while looking over the map. "I didn't realize how big 10,000 acres is. Look at the pond just down from the house. It looks as if it's half a football field. In fact, the water on the map is moving and glittering like the water does in the sunshine. Oh my!"

"What?" Scottie interrupted.

"The map is showing the wooden dock that Pa's building next to the pond so we can run and jump into the water easier. Another plank of wood was just added to Maptrixter!"

"Trixter sure lets us see things as they really do happen on the ranch," Scottie said in amazement.

"Hey, what's this?"

Scottie peered onto Maptrixter and studied where Sophie was pointing. "I'm not sure. It seems to go past the Oak Branch Trail by about a mile by the oak grove. It says that it is the Silver Mineral Mine."

"I didn't know we had an old mine on the ranch," Sophie observed. "I don't think Pa has ever mentioned it."

"Probably because he doesn't want us to know about it and explore it," Scottie figured. "So you know what that means. We have a horse ride to go on today and that ride is to the Silver Mineral Mine!"

"I don't know," Sophie answered. "I think we'd better ask Pa about this first."

"Are you kidding? If we ask Pa about it, he'll say we can't go, or we have to wait for him or Jack to ride with us," Scottie reasoned. "Where is your sense of adventure? Here we have the whole day in front of us with the horses always ready to go on a ride. Besides, we'll have Molly with us, we'll bring our backpacks with some food and water, and we'll be sure to bring Trixter too. So everything will be just fine."

"Okay, I guess you're right. Pa did say that he wanted Molly to go with us on our horse rides," Sophie agreed. "Hey, do you have your rain box in your backpack too?"

Scottie unzipped her pack and under all of her dirty clothes was her rain box as well. She shook it to see if the two quarters were in it, and sure enough both coins were in her box. Scottie decided to put them in her special treasure drawer for safekeeping. These coins had the year that they were born on them, so she knew she should save them. What better place to keep them than in her drawer full of all sorts of treasures she had collected on the ranch. There were beautiful stones, a pretty dead beetle, a brittle but colorful leaf, and even a tiny arrowhead she'd found. She carefully closed the drawer and turned toward Sophie.

"We'd better put our dirty clothes in the wash room," Scottie suggested. "Now, let's hurry so we can feed Fuzzy, pack a lunch, and then get the horses saddled up after breakfast."

After Sophie and Scottie fed Fuzzy and cleaned her pen, they headed back to the kitchen to eat their breakfast and help Ma with the dishes.

"What are you two girls up to today?" Ma asked as she noticed Sophie and Scottie packing a lunch once the breakfast dishes were cleaned up.

"We just finished with Fuzzy, so today is a perfect day to bring Molly along on a horse ride with us," Scottie answered.

"Yeah," Sophie agreed, "we decided that Molly needs to get to know the ranch as soon as possible."

"I see," Ma observed. "Well here, pack up some apples too and here are some chocolate chip cookies that I made yesterday."

"You're the best, Ma," the girls said at the same time as they packed their lunches into the backpacks.

"Where did you get those backpacks?" Ma asked in a puzzled voice.

It just occurred to the girls that Ma hadn't seen the packs before because they got them after walking through the frame from Dr. Drake. Now, they couldn't lie about who gave the packs to them.

"We got them from Dr. Drake when he visited," Sophie quickly answered.

"Yeah, he left them next to the front door and when we went to our rooms we noticed them," Scottie added. "Each one has our name on it. We need to be sure and thank him."

"How thoughtful of him," Ma said with a smile. "Have a good ride, girls. Be safe."

"We will, Ma," Sophie said as they walked out the door toward the stables.

"Whew, that was close," Scottie said shaking her head.

"I know," Sophie agreed. "How could we explain to

27

Ma that Dr. Drake gave us these backpacks in Mexico?"

"She would never believe that story *and* she would never let us walk through that magical frame again!" Scottie almost shouted.

As the girls were walking toward the stables, Pa waved at them from the pond, signaling Sophie and Scottie to inspect his handy work.

"Look, girls. Your swimming dock is just about finished," Pa said proudly.

As the girls walked onto the wood planks, their cowboy boots clicked at every step. They seemed to walk for about ten yards until the planks were over the water. Sophie looked around and thought that Maptrixter was right to show the pond being about half a football field.

"This is great, Pa!" Scottie observed excitedly. "It feels weird to walk out here in boots though. Next time we'll be in sandals and ready for a swim."

"Where are you two off to with Molly?" Pa asked.

Sophie answered first. "We're going on a horse ride because it's time to show Molly around the ranch."

"Well, it's a great day for it," Pa replied. "Just be sure to stay on the main trails and be back before it gets too late. Oh, and did you two feed Fuzzy Mamma and clean her pen?"

"We sure did, Pa," the girls answered at the same time.

They gave Pa a kiss on the cheek and walked back toward the stables and corrals. Once Starburst and Firefly were brushed, each girl put on the horse's blanket and saddle. They talked gently to the horses to keep them calm as they did this. After the girls had cinched the straps of the saddle up tight, they took off the halter that the rope was clipped to and replaced it with the bridle, being very gentle as the bit slipped into the horse's mouth. The girls then led each horse out of the stable and next to a two-foot-long bench. They took turns standing on the bench, where each girl put her left foot into the left stirrup of the saddle. With both hands, Sophie or Scottie would hold onto the horn of the saddle and pull herself up, swinging her right leg over the horse to easily sit on the saddle. It was a little bit trickier with their backpacks on, but the girls managed fine and were ready to go, heading for the Oak Branch Trail and the Silver Mineral Mine.

"Click, click," Sophie sounded with her tongue to Firefly to let her know it was time to get walking away from the stables and toward the trail.

"Come on, Molly," Scottie shouted as Molly relaxed in the shade, watching a beetle walk just in front of her paws where she was laying. Immediately, Molly got up and ran behind the horses as they trotted toward the old silver mine.

As the girls were on the trail heading for the oak grove that Maptrixter had shown, Molly kept on racing after the squirrels and rabbits that would come out of a bush and run to safety in their burrows. Molly's antics made the girls laugh. Sophie pointed to a beautiful blue bird that was busy building its nest. There was a great stretch of trail that was perfect for galloping the horses, so off the horses went, racing each other without either rider encouraging her horse. Molly kept up with them pretty well, which impressed the girls and the horses!

"Whoa, whoa," Scottie said as she pulled back on the reins to get Starburst to slow down and walk. "This must be the oak grove, and according to Trixter, the mine should be just beyond these trees."

"Let's ride over there," Sophie said pointing toward a rather overgrown trail. "It looks as if that trail was used a lot at one time so maybe that will lead us to the mine."

"Well, something is over there," Scottie noticed. "Look at Molly. She is sniffing something in the air and is walking, no, running that way."

"Molly, come back here!" Sophie shouted.

But Molly quickly was out of sight through the weeds on the trail that wound through the trees.

"We'd better follow her as fast as possible," Scottie announced.

Both girls made clicking noises and the horses started to trot on the trail in the direction that Molly ran. Soon they could hear Molly barking.

The horses slowed to a walk as they reached the edge of the grove and into a clearing. The girls could see a half-boarded-up opening that blocked what looked like an archway of rocks.

"This must be the entrance to the silver mine," Scottie stated.

Molly kept running into the entrance of the mine, and then after a little while, she'd run out again, barking almost the entire time.

"There is something in that mine that's really bothering Molly. We'd better investigate," Scottie ordered.

"First, let's tie up the horses and look around

to make sure it's safe before we just go in there," Sophie answered. "I want to get my flashlight out of my backpack too."

"Great thinking, sis!" Scottie proclaimed. "I didn't even think to bring one and of course it's going to be dark in there."

"What a surprise," Sophie replied in a sarcastic tone.

After the girls tied up their horses, they continued to walk to the left of the entrance of the mine. Because the area on the right side of the mine was a hillside full of rocks, they walked to the left, which was covered with loose gravel and more rocks.

"What's that?" Scottie wondered, catching her breath.

Sophie looked closer and Molly was running back and forth from rock to rock. "I think it's fur and those red dots I think are blood. We'd better get out of here," Sophie said guardedly.

Molly then hopped down a little embankment and started to bark again. Scotty followed her and shouted for Sophie to walk toward them. Against Sophie's better judgment, she carefully walked on the rocks to where Scottie was standing. Down just a few rocks below where they stood was what looked like a sleeping dog—not just any dog, a wild dog or perhaps a coyote mix of some kind.

"I don't think she's alive anymore," Sophie stated.

"I don't think so either," Scottie agreed. "How do you know it's a female?"

"Because look, she's nursing," Sophie observed.

Suddenly the girls looked at each other at the same time and shouted "puppies!"

"We need to find them before something happens to them," Scottie announced.

As if Molly could tell what the girls were saying, she quickly started barking and ran back to the entrance of the mine. Both girls quickly followed her and noticed how Molly was able to navigate around the rocks to get through the opening. Each girl had to wait for her eyes to adjust as the sisters cautiously entered into the darkness. The ceiling was low and there were metal tracks on the ground for the once-busy wheeled platform carts that carried the heavy loads of dirt out of the mine.

"Quick, Sophie, take out your flashlight so we can see better," Scottie suggested.

"It's already out, and it is on. Shoot! I don't think it's working. Oh, wait a minute. Here we go. I was pressing the wrong button," Sophie replied with a nervous giggle.

As the girls looked around them, they noticed the tracks were on a narrow dirt-like pathway. The farther they walked, the darker it became in the mine. Suddenly, they saw two glowing eyes coming toward them. They turned around and began to run when they heard a bark and realized it was Molly!

"Whew, thank goodness, it's Molly," Scottie said in a whisper. "We should probably stay close to her."

Sophie nodded and they once again started to follow Molly and the cart tracks. Soon the tracks stopped because of the dirt and rocks that had fallen from the ceiling and walls of the mine.

"We probably shouldn't go any farther," Sophie said. "I don't have a good feeling about this place."

Just as she said that, they could hear something. It was very weak, but something was making a sound.

"Do you hear that?" Scottie asked. "I think it's coming from down there."

The girls followed the brightness cast by the flashlight and could see the trail full of rocks and boulders leading downward. They both suddenly stopped and could see Molly jumping back and forth between two boulders, barking and then whimpering.

"Quiet, Molly!" Scottie shouted.

Now both girls could hear it, a definite high-pitched whimper sound—a sound of puppies.

"We've got to go down there," Scottie stated. "Keep shining the flashlight toward the sound. Those puppies have got to be close."

Just as the girls walked across one of the boulders, they heard the sounds again and looked down. Sure enough, two tiny puppies were lying in a protected crevice of the rocks.

"Oh, how cute," Sophie observed. "It looks like there's only two so we can each put one in our backpacks and bring them home."

"That's a great idea, Sophie," Scottie said with a smile. "How old do you think they are?"

"I'd say about 7 to 10 days, not very old at all," Sophie guessed.

Just as they lifted the puppies up and began to cradle them, Sophie heard another whimpering sound. She quickly looked at Molly and realized that sound didn't come from her.

"Wait, I think I hear another puppy," Sophie said

as she pointed the flashlight a little farther down the trail. "There it is again. Here, take this one and I'm going to check."

As she walked a little more, she saw another puppy with its head barely lifted up, trying to find its mama for food.

"Oh, don't be afraid. We'll take care of you," Sophie said softly as she picked it up.

"Come on, Sophie, hurry up. We need to get these puppies back home," Scottie shouted.

Sophie turned to walk back up the boulder and then darkness!

"Oh no, what happened to the light?" Scottie almost screamed.

"I don't know. I'm pushing all of the buttons on this thing!" Sophie screamed back, causing the puppies to whimper very loudly now.

Then suddenly Sophie calmed down and said, "Here we go. Now we can see."

"What are you talking about?" Scottie asked. "I can't see a thing. Oh, my gosh, your eyes must be kicking in like they did in Mexico and now you can see in the dark!"

"Thank goodness," Sophie answered. "Put your puppies into your backpack and then hold onto my pack as we walk out of here. I'll tell you where to step and how high to step over a rock."

So both girls very carefully walked up the path. Soon Scottie could feel the rails on the ground as they got closer to the entrance. The sunlight was barely shining through the old boards under the rock archway, which made it light enough to see. Now

Scottie could see Sophie and her eyes, which looked like a cat's. Scottie thought that she would never get used to that.

"Boy, that was close," Sophie said, referring to the danger in the mine.

The girls quickly ran to where the horses were tethered and pulled the puppies out of their backpacks. They were so little and weak. Both girls sat down with Molly, who was constantly trying to sniff and lick the puppies.

"With the way Molly is acting, you'd think the puppies were hers," Scottie said as she watched Molly constantly trying to give the puppies a bath.

The girls took out their water, each cupping her hand to catch the water for the puppies to drink. After a while, all three puppies slurped up the water, sucking on the girls' fingers as they tried to get more.

Realizing that they had not eaten lunch yet, the girls quickly ate their sandwiches, apples, and cookies. Carefully, Scottie put two of the puppies in her backpack. She turned the pack around so it was in front of her. She looked at Sophie to make sure her eyes went back to normal and then found a boulder to lead Starburst next to. Scottie climbed up the boulder and easily swung her leg over the saddle to sit securely on her horse. The puppies whimpered a little and then settled down.

"What a smart idea," Sophie said in an impressed voice and did the same. "Let's head for home. Come on, Molly. Let's go, girl."

Molly quickly smelled the scent of the puppies in the air and stayed as close as possible to the horses as they turned back onto the trail toward the ranch house.

CHAPTER THREE

Plan on It!

Soon the girls were on the Oak Branch Trail riding toward the ranch house. The sun was still shining and the girls couldn't wait to show Ma and Pa what they had found.

"These puppies are so cute!" Scottie said with a giggle as she peered into her backpack in front of her. The pack rested quite nicely on the shoulders of Starburst, just in front of the horn of the saddle.

"They sure are sweet," Sophie agreed. "I think I'll call this one Shadow since he was on his own down the rocky path of the mine in the shadows."

"That's a good name for him," Scottie replied. "You know what's kind of neat about these puppies, too, is that they have an instant mother. Did you notice how Molly is acting? It's as if she was their mother all along."

"I know it's neat. I hope that her milk will come in like surrogate mothers of other animals. Then I'm positive these puppies will survive," Sophie said in an informative way.

As the girls got closer to the stables, Scottie decided to gallop Starburst almost the rest of the way. This, of course, made Firefly want to gallop too. The girls were careful not to upset the puppies, and the horses were soon side by side on the trail that turned into a dirt road.

"Whoa, whoa," Sophie said with authority to Firefly as they reached the stables.

Each girl carefully got off her horse and set her backpack gently on the ground.

"How was your ride, girls?" Jack asked, noticing a sound coming from the backpacks.

"Look, Jack! Look what we found!" Scottie said while leading Starburst into her corral.

Sophie had already put Firefly in the corral and ran over to open her pack wide enough for Jack to peek inside.

"Well, I'll be. Puppies. Where did you two find them?"

"In the old silver mine off of the Oak Branch Trail by the oak grove," Sophie answered. As she lifted Shadow out of her pack to give Jack a closer look, Molly ran over and jumped up to see Shadow.

"You'd better go show your parents what you found, but I'm not so sure you should tell them where you found the puppies. I don't think your Pa would've wanted you two to go near that old mine without him or me. Good luck, girls. I'll go ahead and take the saddles and bridles off the horses."

"Thanks, Jack. Ma and Pa won't be able to resist them, no matter where we found them!" Scottie said. She carefully picked up her backpack and headed up to the house with Sophie.

Molly was running around each girl as they walked up to the house, not wanting to let the puppies out of her sight.

As Scottie opened the door to the screened-in porch, Ma came into the small room from the kitchen.

"So, girls, how was your ride?" Ma asked. "You two seemed to be gone quite a long time."

"Look, Ma! Look what we found!" the girls yelled at the same time with huge grins on their faces.

Just as they opened the packs and showed Ma, Pa walked into the room. Molly kept circling around the girls with her tail wagging and whimpering at the same time.

"Well, look what we've got here," Pa said as the girls pulled each puppy out of the packs.

"Oh, my," Ma said while quickly getting two towels from one of the nearby cabinets for the puppies to lie on. "Where on earth did you find these precious puppies?"

"In the old mine beyond the oak grove," Scottie blurted out.

"You went to the old silver mine?" Pa asked with concern in his voice. "I didn't even know you girls knew about it. In fact, I haven't mentioned it so you wouldn't go in there. Now I know to talk to you two about what is off limits on this ranch!" Pa continued in an irritated tone.

"We didn't have any intentions of going in, but Molly was acting crazy, going in and out of the half-boarded-up entrance barking and whimpering," Sophie explained.

"Yes, and once we noticed the animal fur and blood, we quickly spotted the coyote-mix dog that wasn't breathing anymore," Scottie added. "We figured she must have died while trying to protect something."

"That's when I noticed that she had been nursing and puppies were probably what Molly was barking at," Sophie added.

"Well, that doesn't sound safe at all, with a dead animal near you girls, but I guess you two couldn't very well have left the puppies in there," Ma stated as she lifted Shadow up and petted its soft puppy fur.

"Okay, before we all get too attached to these little ones," Pa said, "I want to check your back-packs for any flees or other bugs that might infest the porch or Molly. I see that she is quite taken with the puppies already."

Sophie quickly took Maptrixter out of the pack so Ma and Pa wouldn't ask where she got the map. Pa inspected the packs and gave the okay for the puppies to stay on the porch with Molly. Ma quickly got some milk from the kitchen and a dropper so the puppies could eat.

"Let's get them on Molly after they eat to see if this will activate her milk to come in," Ma suggested as the girls just looked on in wonder.

"Alright, girls, go feed Fuzzy Mama and her baby and then come on back to get washed up for dinner.

40

We have some news that I think you'll like," Pa said with a wink and a grin.

After Sophie and Scottie were done with their chores, they quickly ran up to the house to check on Molly and the puppies. All of them were on the towels that Ma had put on the floor of the porch for them, fast asleep. They both got washed up for dinner, helped Ma set the table, and waited for Pa to come in. They could smell Ma's yummy lasagna in the oven and couldn't wait to eat it for dinner. While the girls sat at the table, they noticed that the kitchen had all sorts of lists taped to the cabinets above the counters. One was a list of guests, another a menu of food items for a party or something, and another was an itemized food list.

"Hey, Ma," Scottie began, "what are all of these lists for?"

"These lists are what your Pa wants to talk to you girls about," Ma answered.

Soon Pa came into the kitchen, sat down, and was ready to eat. He looked at the girls after he said grace to thank the Lord for their food and said, "I have an announcement. This Saturday we are hosting a wedding."

"A wedding!" the girls blurted out.

"Wow," Sophie replied, "we've never been to a wedding before. Who is getting married?"

"Remember meeting Dr. Drake the other day?" Pa began to explain as the girls nodded yes.

"Well, he came here to ask us if we could host his and your Aunt Jill's wedding here."

"I didn't even know they were engaged!" Scottie exclaimed

"Yes, this will be quite an event," Ma said with a smile. "Therefore, I am going to need your help, girls. And Auntie Jill would like you two to be junior bridesmaids in the ceremony."

"How exciting!" Sophie said while clapping.

"Does this mean we have to get all fancy in a frilly dress?" Scottie asked, rolling her eyes.

"Yes, it does," Ma answered. "The dresses are beautiful but not too 'frilly' as you put it, Scottie. In fact, I have them hanging up in each of your closets in your room. I would like you to try them on after dinner to make sure they fit."

"Where on the ranch is the wedding going to be?" Sophie asked.

"In the old stone house on the other side of the pond," Ma explained. "It's the perfect location because we can set up the tables, chairs, and all of the food in the old house. The ceremony will be outside under the ancient oak tree. Pa has already started to hang the chandeliers from the giant branches so there will be plenty of light."

By the tone of her voice, the girls could tell that Ma was really excited about the wedding. After helping Ma with the dishes, the girls quickly ran to their room to inspect their new dresses.

"Oh, look how beautiful they are!" Sophie exclaimed as she held the dress up to her and twirled around in front of the mirror.

"Well, I guess it's okay," Scottie said while inspecting the dress.

Sophie's dress was light green with satin material and covered with a lighter green sheer material over the satin. It had lace along the rounded neck in the same light green with a blue ribbon around the bodice, just above the waist. It was sleeveless, which was perfect for the warm summer evenings. Scottie's dress was similar but in light blue material and with a green ribbon on the dress.The length of both dresses went just below their knees.

"Look how perfect it fits," Sophie admired as she looked and turned in front of the mirror.

"Well, I guess they look okay," Scottie agreed, looking in front of her mirror.

Just as the girls were admiring their new dresses, they noticed the frame's crystals were flashing bright colors.

"I think the frame is happy that Dr. Drake and Auntie Jill are getting married. I also think that it likes my dress best!" Scottie teased as she walked over to pick up the frame and watch the colors flashing.

Soon there was a knock on the door and Ma walked in. The frame instantly turned to its original silver and clear sparkly color.

"Oh, girls," Ma said almost breathlessly, "the dresses look perfect and I see you found the matching shoes. Auntie Jill is going to love it. Now I am going to be really busy in the next few days with the food and all. Auntie Jill has really planned everything, so you girls will see her the morning of the wedding."

"That's fine, Ma. We promise to take care of the puppies and do our chores without needing to be reminded," Sophie said and then looked at Scottie to make sure she agreed.

The next morning, the girls could tell that it was going to be a very warm day.

"Let's go swimming in the pond today," Scottie suggested.

"That's a great idea," Sophie agreed. "Let's be sure to bring Molly. She could use a break from the puppies and it would be good for her to cool down with that thick fur of hers."

After they ate breakfast and did their chores, the girls headed down the dirt road from the ranch house toward the pond. Each had a towel, and Sophie also had swimming goggles, water shoes, and sun screen.

"Boy, Sophie, are you sure you need all that stuff?" Scottie asked.

"Yes, I'm sure!" Sophie replied while almost marching to the pond. "Now get the snacks and let's go. Come on, Molly, let's go cool off."

As the girls walked onto the new wooden dock, Molly carefully walked next to them, stopping every now and then to look at the water through the space between the boards.

"I think Molly is a little nervous on these boards," Scottie noticed.

"Is Molly afraid of the water?" Sophie asked as they got to the end of the dock and carefully peered over the edge to look at the water. "This must be 10 feet deep. I can barely see the bottom of the pond."

Just then, Scottie walked over to Sophie and pretended to push her in the water, grabbing her just before she lost her footing completely. Molly began to scold Scottie with a lot of barking!

"Very funny, Scottie," Sophie yelled and she quickly stepped back from the edge.

"Oh, come on, I was just playing around. I'd never push you in," Scottie laughed.

After the girls set their stuff down Scottie said, "Okay, let's link arms and run and jump in. Maybe Molly will join us if we both go in at once."

Sophie put on her water shoes and agreed. They walked back about 20 feet and ran down the dock at full speed. Splash! The girls were in the water. Molly wasn't sure what to do, so she barked and barked out of excitement and irritation for the girls. Once she realized that there wasn't any danger, she jumped right in with a huge splash. The girls laughed and laughed.

Sophie and Scottie found the wood ladder that Pa had attached to the dock, climbing up it as fast as possible and then jumping off the edge over and over. Pa saw them and waved, laughing at the fun they were having. Molly used the sandy bank of the pond to get out of the water and run around the edge of the pond toward the dock to greet the girls, splashing them with her wet fur when she'd shake to dry off. After jumping off the dock several times, Sophie and Scottie decided to rest a while on their towels on the warm wooden boards of the dock.

"Ugh! Molly, you're getting us all wet!" Sophie yelled and laughed at the same time as Molly shook her fur right next to her as she lay on her towel.

"This is perfect," Scottie giggled as she rearranged her crumpled towel after Molly messed it up while trying to lick Scottie dry.

"I know," Sophie agreed while eating her snack. "Look at the old stone house. The chairs and tables are being delivered. I can't wait to see Auntie Jill and Dr. Drake all fancied up at their wedding ceremony."

"I'm excited too," Scottie agreed. "I'm even okay with wearing that dress in the wedding. I mean, it's only for a few hours and what could go wrong?"

"What do you mean, what could go wrong?" Sophie asked.

"Well, you know me and getting dressed up. It seems that I always spill something on my clothes or trip and scuff up my shoes. But this time, I'm going to be extra careful so I don't ruin my clothes for their wedding ceremony," Scottie said in a determined voice.

After their snack break, the girls went back in the water and Molly ran up to the house to be with the puppies. Once the girls felt comfortable in the pond, Pa brought them a small boat that could easily be tied up next to the ladder for them to use any time they wanted. In fact, each day after their chores, both girls would swim in the pond daily for the rest of the week. Molly's milk finally came in, so she was with the puppies a lot more than with the girls.

"Oh look," Sophie noticed as the puppies began to suckle on Molly again on the day before the wedding. "I'm so glad that Molly can feed them and we don't have to. I can see how Shadow has really grown and is ready to explore outside."

"Yes, we'll have to be careful about closing the screen door to make sure the puppies don't get out when we're not looking," Ma said as she put all sorts of food items in their giant freezer.

Both girls agreed and played with the puppies on the porch floor after dinner.

"Whew, it's late," Ma said. "Let's all turn in for the night. We have an early day tomorrow for last-minute details before the wedding begins at 3:00 in the afternoon. Auntie Jill will be here for breakfast, so we can talk about when you girls walk down the aisle before she does."

Sophie and Scottie kissed Ma goodnight and headed for their room.

The sound of Ma laughing in the kitchen woke the girls up very early in the morning, just after sunrise. After they dressed and brushed their hair, they quickly walked into the kitchen.

"Auntie Jill!" both shouted at the same time.

"Sophie, Scottie, you two are finally up," Auntie Jill teased as she gave both of them a hug. "Are you both ready to be in my wedding?"

The girls nodded as they hugged her back.

"We want to thank you again for the beautiful frame that you gave us. It makes all of the pictures that are put in it almost come to life!" Sophie said as she looked at Scottie and then back to Auntie Jill.

"Well, I'm glad you like it. They're very rare you know," Auntie Jill replied, "only a few like them in the world."

"Oh, wow," Scottie said in amazement, "we'll take extra good care of it."

"I'm sure you two will," Ma interrupted. "Now girls

go down to the barn and tend to Fuzzy Mama and then hurry back up to the house. You two need to eat breakfast and then I need to style your hair for the ceremony."

"Okay, Ma. Hey what happened to Molly and the puppies?" Scottie asked after looking into the porch from the kitchen.

"Oh, Jack made an outdoor dog house for them with a little fence around it so the puppies can run around easier to sniff and play. Molly has a special doggy ramp that allows her to get in and out without the puppies being able to follow her," Ma answered as she poured Auntie Jill more coffee.

"This is cool!" Scottie said as they walked out of the porch to observe Jack's handy work. "I'm not sure how long it will take for one of the puppies to figure out that ramp though. Shadow seems really smart and independent."

"I think you're right," Sophie agreed while checking out the puppy play area.

The girls then continued to walk down to the barn to do their chores and to get back to the house for food and beautification!

"Hold still, Scottie!" Ma ordered as she continued to brush her long wavy red hair. "I will be done with your hair as soon as I can brush your tangles out and put the front of your hair back into this beautiful barrette that Auntie Jill gave you. In fact, I'm not sure what kind of stones these are," Ma continued while inspecting the hair barrette, "but it is beautiful. The stones seem to pick up the exact color of your blue dress."

"Yeah, settle down, Scottie, so Ma can do my hair.

These barrettes are beautiful," Sophie said.

Soon, each sister's hair was done and all they needed to do was to put on their dresses, lace socks, and shoes.

"I want you girls to be very careful after you put these dresses on so you don't get them wrinkled or dirty," Ma said as she lifted one of the dresses out of the closet to inspect it for any last-minute ironing needs. "You two will get a ride with Jack to the stone house by 2:30, so be sure to be in front of the house at that time. Now, it's my turn to get ready for this wonderful wedding," Ma said as she left the room.

"Oh darn," Sophie began, "I wanted Ma to curl the ends of my hair before I put on my dress. I'll meet you out front, Scottie, as soon as I'm done."

"Okay," Scottie said with a sigh as she looked at her dress, trying to figure out how best to put it on without wrinkling it. "I have some time, so I might as well go play with the puppies for a few minutes."

Scottie sat in the middle of the new puppy pen as they pounced and climbed all over her. She couldn't help but laugh and laugh. A couple of times she had to scold Shadow for biting her a little too hard.

"Ouch!" Scottie shouted at Shadow as she picked him up and had his cute fluffy face right in front of hers, almost nose to nose. "You have needle teeth that are very sharp!"

Shadow then wriggled out of her hands and started to bark at her while running around her and the other two puppies, as if trying to say catch me if you can. Soon Scottie got up to walk out of the pen to get on her dress and finish getting ready for the wedding, not realizing the latch to the gate wasn't completely closed.

CHAPTER FOUR

Drip! Drip! Drip!

Once Scottie put her dress on, she couldn't help but admire herself in the mirror. Her hair looked really pretty pulled back and her waves made the ends curl naturally. With her shoes and socks on, she left the bedroom and went outside to wait for Sophie and Jack. As she sat on the bench next to the front door, Scottie noticed a lot of barking coming from the dock of the pond. She thought it was strange that Molly would be there and not in the pen with her puppies.

"Oh, no!" Scottie shouted as she began to run toward the pond.

"Are you almost done, Ma?" Sophie asked. "I want to go outside with Scottie and wait for Jack."

"Let me just curl this last section. Okay, your hair is done and it looks perfect!" Ma observed.

Quickly, Sophie left Ma to go outside. She wasn't sure why, but she knew something was terribly wrong and had to find Scottie right away. As Sophie stepped outside the house, she looked around for her sister and saw the back of her dress as she ran on the dock.

"The puppies, the puppies!" Scottie yelled. She ran as fast as she could, but began to slip and slide on the smooth wood planks of the dock as if she were on a sheet of ice. Her slick leather-soled shoes continued to slide, her arms made full backward motioned circles on each side of her, and then SPLASH!

"Stop, Scottie!" Sophie shouted, but it was too late. Scottie in her beautiful dress and fancy shoes was now in the pond.

Molly was pacing back and forth on the dock, barking louder than ever. She couldn't take it any longer and jumped into the water, trying to reach Scottie and Shadow.

Sophie ran toward the pond and was soon peering over the edge of the dock. She watched as Scottie swam to a clump of oak branches and leaves that Shadow was tangled in. Sophie was pretty amazed how Scottie was able to swim over to Shadow without getting her entire head wet.

"Quick, Sophie, get in the boat and row over here and help me. I think Molly is going to make things worse, so call her over to you too," Scottie ordered.

"Hold on. I'm coming as fast as I can. Come on, Molly. It's okay. Come on. That's a good girl," Sophie coaxed Molly while reaching for the boat.

Quickly, Sophie climbed into the boat, but as she reached for the oars, the right shoulder of her dress got snagged on one of the nails of the dock. Soon she was right next to Scottie.

"Oh, no you don't, Shadow," Scottie said as she grabbed the puppy from sinking under the water. "Now you're safe, little one," she continued as she carefully handed Shadow to Sophie.

Sophie put Shadow on the bottom of the boat and tried to help Scottie into it as well.

"Stop, Sophie. It's no use. The boat is rocking too much and I don't want to tip it over into the pond. I'll just hold on from the side while you row us back to the dock."

As soon as they got back, Scottie climbed up the ladder attached to the dock and took off her shoes and socks to start the drying process. Molly kept licking Shadow after Sophie put him on the dock. The puppy was whimpering, but Sophie could tell that he would be just fine.

"Gosh, Scottie, thank goodness you noticed Molly barking. I wonder how Shadow got out of the pen," Sophie said as she watched Molly.

"I don't know, but let's run back to the house to put Shadow back and I'm going to need your help to dry off," Scottie answered in almost a panic. "Jack will be here any minute, so let's run!"

Sophie carefully put Shadow back into the pen with Molly right behind her and noticed that the door latch wasn't closed properly. She closed the pen door, checking it carefully, and then she and Scottie, who was still holding her shoes and socks, ran into the house.

"Okay, I have an idea," Sophie said as she let Scottie into Ma's bathroom. "Get into the tub and I'll use the hair dryer to dry your dress. I figure if it can dry Ma's hair fast, it should dry your dress too. I think the outer sheer part will dry quickly, but the satin part will just have to do. I can't believe that your shoes stayed on your feet while you were in the water. Luckily, they are patent leather and look kind of wet anyways."

HONK, HONK!

"Oh, no, Jack's out front in the truck. Hurry, Sophie, and help me out of the tub so I can put on my socks and shoes," Scottie ordered as she was trying to get out of the bathtub without slipping. "Check my hair too. Does the barrette look okay?"

"Everything looks fine," Sophie observed. "I don't think anyone will even notice that your dress is still wet. Now we've got to go meet Jack before he comes into the house looking for us!"

"Come on, girls. If we're late, I'll never hear the end of it from your Pa," Jack said as he motioned the girls to get into the front of the truck.

"No, I'll ride in the back," Scottie said as she got into the bed of the truck, sitting on her knees to get the dress to dry more in the breeze as they headed for the old stone house.

Ma was looking back from her seat in the front row of the chairs, trying to find Sophie and Scottie. She let out a sigh of relief as she saw them standing there with their basket of flowers, ready to walk down the aisle when the music started.

"Can you tell I snagged my dress?" Sophie asked Scottie.

"You're worried about that? Oh, my gosh, Sophie, you make me laugh," Scottie replied as she looked down and could see a little puddle forming around her!

"Okay, girls, the music has started so you can walk down the aisle now," Auntie Jill whispered loudly to them.

They did not notice that Auntie Jill was standing there and almost jumped out of their shoes! They both gasped at how beautiful she looked in her wedding gown and then smiled as they began to walk toward where Dr. Drake and Pa were standing.

Soon all were at the front of the guests, with everyone looking at Auntie Jill. Ma was smiling and then her eyes became really big. Pa looked over to see what she was staring at and began to chuckle a little. The puddle around Scottie was pretty big. Sophie began to giggle and Scottie just rolled her eyes.

Dr. Drake and Auntie Jill shook their heads with a smile and the ceremony continued as planned.

"This wedding cake is really good," Scottie said after taking a large bite and looking at her dress. "I think my dress is dry now. I don't think anyone noticed while we took pictures."

"I don't see a puddle where you're sitting, so I guess you're right," Sophie agreed before she took a bite of cake too.

"Are you two having a nice time?" Dr. Drake asked, pulling up a chair to sit next to the girls.

Both nodded with a smile.

"It sounds like you two have been having some adventures here at the ranch. In fact, you both may be ready for another adventure soon," Dr. Drake said with a wink and then went to talk with guests at another table.

"Uh oh, here come Ma and Pa," Scottie said while nudging Sophie.

"You two did a great job!" Pa said as he bent over to kiss each one on the top of her head.

"But I don't know why you were dripping wet, Scarlet," Ma said and then turned to Sophie. "And I don't know why your dress is snagged. I won't ask questions but I want you girls to spend your day tomorrow in your room to clean it from top to bottom. I hope this 'quiet' time will help you to think about your actions in the future."

Then Ma and Pa walked away, leaving the girls to let out a big sigh.

"Boy, I think we were lucky with that punishment," Sophie said after finishing her cake. "You always know Ma is serious when she calls you Scarlet. Let's head up to the house to make sure the puppies are okay and get out of these clothes."

"Good idea," Scottie agreed while standing up and waving goodbye to Auntie Jill and Dr. Drake. "Did you notice how Dr. Drake winked at us after saying we may be ready for another adventure?"

"Yeah, I guess," Sophie answered. "Should we ask Jack for a ride back to the house?"

"No, I'd rather walk. I was thinking," Scottie continued, "we might want to ask Ma for that envelope when we're done cleaning our room."

"That's a good idea. I'm curious where Ma decided to hide the envelope," Sophie said as they started to walk on the dirt road toward the house.

"Ah, back into shorts and a t-shirt," Scottie said. She put her dress into the dirty clothes hamper and then continued, "I'm going to check on Molly and the puppies. Thank goodness, only one puppy got out of the pen."

"Okay, I'll be there in a minute," Sophie answered. "I think I'll make a sandwich. Do you want one?"

"Sure, I don't think Ma and Pa will be back to the house from the wedding reception for a while and I'm hungry too."

The puppies were fine. Scottie fed Molly, and when she got back to the kitchen a nice turkey and cheese sandwich was waiting for her.

"Gosh, Sophie, this is really a good sandwich. Why are you being so nice to me?"

"Well, I figured you earned it by saving Shadow," Sophie replied after taking a bite of her sandwich.

"Gosh, I don't think I can eat another bite," Scottie said after drinking some milk and pushing her almost eaten sandwich away from her.

"I know. I'm full too. Let's clean up our mess and go to bed. I can barely keep from yawning."

Scottie agreed and once the dishes were cleaned up, the girls headed to their room, got ready for bed, and were soon fast asleep.

CHAPTER FIVE

Auntie's Instructions

"Wake up, wake up girls," Ma said to them as they were still sleeping in their beds. "You two need to get up and start your day of animal chores and then clean your room."

"Ah, Ma," Scottie began to whine.

"A deal is a deal girls. Let's go. I've got breakfast waiting to give you two energy for this exciting day of cleaning and organizing," Ma continued in a teasing way.

"Organizing too?" Sophie chimed in with a yawn.

"Yes, organizing too," Ma said with a smile and left the room.

"Well, I guess my closet is a mess," Scottie commented out loud as she looked around inside it.

After breakfast and feeding Fuzzy and her baby, the girls got to work, scrubbing their bathroom, vacuuming the floors, dusting the shelves, and washing their window. The hard part was to come—organizing their closets.

While Scottie was hard at work, Sophie decided to take a break and check on the puppies. Once she got back to their bedroom, she noticed the frame was glowing many colors, rotating in a circular motion around the frame. When Sophie picked it up, the frame instantly calmed down and changed to a beautiful teal blue. First, it was very bright and then it became a lighter color, going back and forth as if it was purring!

"Gosh, the frame seems really restless today," Sophie observed while holding the frame with a firm grip to make sure she didn't drop it.

Scottie walked over to look at the frame as it was purring blue colors in Sophie's hand. "Let me see what colors it will turn to if I hold it," Scottie said and tried to grab it from Sophie.

"Stop, Scottie!" Sophie ordered, gripping the frame harder.

"Oh, come on, you've been holding the frame for a long time. Now it's my turn!" Scottie replied in a loud and whining voice.

Sophie gripped the frame even harder and, suddenly, both girls heard a loud and almost shrill "snap"! Each sister looked in horror as each held one-half of the frame in her hand. Instantly, they put the frame halves down on the oak table and ran to their own beds, putting their faces in their pillows. Sophie just stared at nothing.

"I can't (sob) believe we just broke one of the most important gifts we've ever received," Scottie said in a shaky voice.

"I don't know how we can tell Auntie Jill about the frame. She'll be so disappointed in us," Sophie answered with a heavy sigh.

"Maybe we can fix it. I know Pa has some really sticky glue in his workshop we could try to use," Scottie suggested.

"We don't even know how the frame works and I'm afraid if we touched it, it would just make it worse," Sophie answered in a calm and sad voice.

"Well, I'm just trying to find a way to get it to work again!" Scottie said and began to cry again.

"I know, but crying isn't going to solve anything," Sophie said while walking over to Scottie's bed to give her a hug and wipe away her own tears.

"I'm sorry, sis," Scottie apologized. "I should've waited for you to be done looking at the frame."

"That's okay. You get a little more excited over things than I do I guess," Sophie answered.

Suddenly, between sobs, Scottie heard something.

"Did you hear that?" Scottie asked in between sniffs as she looked toward the oak table.

"Hear what?" Sophie asked while wiping away another tear.

Clackity, clackity, clackity was the sound, almost as if something was clapping and drumming really fast on the table. Both girls focused on the frame halves. Each side of the frame was moving back and forth in a hopping fashion. Faster and faster the

61

frame pieces tapped, like a drummer in a parade. As the girls watched, the frame began to rise from the table. Now each half was swirling around the other faster and faster like a tornado. Then the girls heard a loud click! The silence that followed was almost deafening as the girls jumped off Scottie's bed and ran over to the table. The frame was still hovering, rapidly changing colors. The crystals were blue, then orange, yellow, red, green, purple, and back to blue again. Then it finally went thud onto the oak table, silent and purring again in teal blue and light blue. Both girls reached for the frame, and then Scottie quickly removed her hand as Sophie picked it up.

"It looks good as new!" Sophie exclaimed.

"Whew, that was a close one," Scottie sighed.

"From now on, we need to be more patient with one another," Sophie said as she handed Scottie the frame.

"I agree," Scottie said with a smile as she now inspected the frame. "I think we need to get the envelope from Ma and see where the frame wants us to go to next."

"Well, the room looks clean to me, so let's go ask Ma where it is," Sophie suggested while Scottie gently put the frame back on the round table.

The girls looked over the room and their closet and then set out to find Ma, who was in the kitchen making thick buttermilk biscuits.

"Hmm, Ma, those biscuits sure smell good," Scottie said, smelling the cooling biscuits on the kitchen counter.

"Is your room ready for my inspection?" Ma asked as she put another tray into the oven.

"Yep, the room is ready to go," Sophie enthusiastically answered. "In fact, we're also ready for the envelope that you're holding for us."

"What envelop, dear?" Ma asked Sophie.

"You know," Scottie reminded Ma, "the envelope that Auntie Jill sent us a few weeks ago. We asked you to put it in a safe place for us and we'd open it up later."

"Oh, yes, that envelope. Hmm, let's see. Where *did* I put that?" Ma said more to herself than to the girls.

"Now, Ma, don't tell us you put it in such a good hiding place that you can't remember where you put it!" Scottie said in an almost panicked tone.

"Oh, don't worry. I'm sure it will come to me. You know, with the wedding and all, I kind of lost track of some things," Ma replied.

"That's okay, Ma," Sophie encouraged. "I know you'll find it. Maybe we can help."

"Yeah, Ma, let's recreate your steps to where you think you might've put it," Scottie said while walking around the kitchen and looking in cupboards and bookshelves.

"No, not there," Ma said while watching Scottie. "I know I started to put the groceries away for the wedding so I went over here to the pantry."

Both girls immediately ran over to the pantry door to open it and carefully stepped inside to inspect all of the shelves, but no envelope.

"Not there, huh?" Ma asked.

The girls shook their heads.

"Okay, then I needed to start some laundry, so I might've put it on the shelf in the laundry room," Ma continued to think out loud.

So both girls ran to the laundry room to see if it was in there, but once again, nothing.

"This is crazy, girls. I know that darn envelope can't be too far. Hmm, I did need to go into the porch for the puppies, I watered some house plants, I...I know!" Ma almost shouted.

Ma then quickly walked to the screened-in porch and headed for the large freezer in the other end of the room. She opened the freezer door and announced, "Ah ha, here it is!"

Carefully, Ma pulled the very cold envelope out of the freezer saying, "I guess you two would've never looked in here for it!"

"Oh, Ma, do you think the picture in it is okay?" Scottie asked in a very concerned voice.

"Oh, sure, it didn't get wet or anything. Just let it get to room temperature and I'm sure it will be fine," Ma assured her.

Sophie took the envelope from Ma and couldn't resist opening it to look inside. To her surprise there were three smaller envelopes inside. She let out a sigh of relief, knowing that whatever was inside the three envelopes was protected by the larger outer one.

"Thanks, Ma," Sophie said and took Scottie's arm as they ran back to their bedroom.

"You're welcome," Ma answered, seeing only the backs of the girls' heads.

When they got back into their room, Scottie looked out into the hallway and then closed the door.

"Oh, my gosh," Scottie said with excitement, "I can't wait to open the envelope."

"You heard what Ma said," Sophie reminded Scottie. "We can't open the envelope until it is at room temperature. Besides, there are three envelopes in it and I don't want to ruin any of them."

"Oh, okay, then let's go check on Fuzzy Mama and make sure she and her baby have enough food and water. Then it should be warm enough to open," Scottie said reluctantly.

As the girls went down to the barn, Molly decided to join them too. The girls usually wouldn't let her into the barn, but since she'd lived on the ranch for a while, they thought it would be all right for her to meet Fuzzy and the baby. At first, Molly didn't know what Fuzzy Mama was and her hair stood straight up on her shoulders and her back. She even let out a growl!

"It's okay, Molly," Scottie said softly while bending down on her knees to pet her. "This is Fuzzy Mama and her baby lamb."

Sophie was already in the pen to give Fuzzy more alfalfa pellets, and Scottie took the watering can to get more water for the water bucket. Molly then figured out that this animal wasn't a dog or a threat to the girls and just lay down on the cool wood floor of the barn, waiting for the girls to finish their chores.

"There, all done," Sophie announced as she smoothed out the fresh straw in Fuzzy's pen. "Last one to the house is a rotten egg!"

Both girls quickly put their rakes away and started to run for the barn door with Molly at their heels, barking the whole way back to the house.

"Hey girls, you forgot to close the barn door!" Jack yelled as the girls were almost at the house.

Sophie got to the screen door of the kitchen first and burst into the room so fast that she almost bumped the warm biscuits off the cookie sheet that Ma was holding.

"Honestly, Sophie," Ma began and then Scottie almost flew into the kitchen as well. "You two need to slow down. I'm too old for this rough housing!" Ma finished in a rather loud and stern voice. "Oh, and girls, I inspected your room and it looks great."

"Thanks, Ma. We'll try to slow down too," both girls said breathlessly and walked quickly out of the kitchen and headed for their bedroom.

The sisters entered the room and ran to pick up the envelope. Sure enough, it was room temperature.

"Now, there are three envelopes in there," Sophie described as they looked at each other while both were holding the envelope. "How do you want to decide who opens up each one?"

"Well, I guess you can open up two and I'll open one since I kind of made us break the frame," Scottie decided as she let go of the envelope.

"That's very fair of you sis, thanks," Sophie said as she sat down on her bed, opened up the envelope, and pulled out three of the smaller envelopes. "It looks like they are numbered one, two, and three. Here I go with opening up the first one."

Sophie pulled a piece of paper out of envelope number one. It had a scene of waves crashing on some rocks in the background.

"This is pretty stationery paper," Sophie observed and then both girls looked at the frame. Its colors were going crazy, constantly changing brighter than they'd ever seen.

"Oh, boy, Sophie, I think the frame is just as excited as we are about the envelopes," Scottie announced. "Now hurry up and read the letter!"

Dear Sophie and Scottie,
Uncle Rusty and I were very proud of how well you worked together in Mexico. The way you helped Uncle Rusty and Diego discover why the monarch butterflies were missing and where they had disappeared to was brilliant! Because of your great work, we would like your help with another mystery. First, you will need to read the instructions in envelope two. Then when you're ready, we mean really ready and have completed everything, you can open envelope three.
We love you,
Auntie Jill and Uncle Rusty

"Oh, my gosh," Sophie exclaimed, "this is so exciting!"

"Okay, now give me the second envelope so I can read the instructions," Scottie ordered while holding out her hand.

Scottie carefully pulled out an 8½ by 11-inch paper from the second envelope. There were several paragraphs on the paper, all numbered in the sequence of when to perform each task. Sophie sat next to Scottie on her bed so they could both read each paragraph together.

"Gosh, according to these instructions, there sure are a lot of things we need to do before we open the third envelope," Sophie commented. "First, we need to remember what was in the backpacks that we used in Mexico and repack all of those items."

"I have a piece of paper so we can start listing everything," Scottie said, sitting at her desk.

Once the list was complete, each girl got to work and began packing the items into her backpack: shorts, tops, sandals, swimsuit, toothbrush, toothpaste, hair brush, socks, undergarments, pajamas, and rain box.

"I don't think we need to pack the rain box," Scottie said after watching Sophie put hers into the backpack.

"I'm going to because it was in our packs in Mexico," Sophie replied. "I'm sure one will be enough if you don't want to pack yours. There's just something special about the boxes that I feel we should always bring at least one on our, uh, trips. Okay, I think that takes care of that task," Sophie observed with a smile.

"Girls, time for dinner," Ma said as she poked her head into their bedroom doorway. "Are you two going somewhere?" she asked as she noticed the backpacks at the foot of each bed.

"We thought that maybe we could go on another horse ride and then pretend to be somewhere far away and camp under the stars in the courtyard," Scottie said quickly.

"Of course, the horses wouldn't camp with us, but we can pretend," Sophie added.

"Oh, alright, that does sound like fun, but not until tomorrow, girls. Now let's eat," Ma said as she picked up the frame to inspect it again. "This really is a beautiful frame. The crystals on it almost seem alive with how sparkly they are."

Scottie let out a rather loud laugh and Sophie elbowed her in the side. Then they took Ma's hand and quickly walked out of their room toward the kitchen and dinner.

"That was an excellent dinner of beef enchiladas, Ma," Pa said while rubbing his full stomach. "Now what do you two girls have in store for this wonderful summer evening?"

"We're going to go down to the stables and brush Starburst and Firefly. We thought we'd go on another ride tomorrow if that's okay with you, Pa," Sophie replied.

"Is that okay, Ma?" Pa asked and she nodded yes. "Then that's fine with me, but no more puppies," Pa said with a smile.

Both girls laughed, gave him a kiss on the cheek, and then headed for the horses.

"Once we get done with grooming the horses, we'll be finished with the second task and it will be really quick to saddle them up tomorrow," Scottie said.

"I know, so let's make sure the bridles and the saddle blankets are clean and ready to go. Then we don't have to fuss with them in the morning," Sophie suggested as Molly came running up beside her.

"We need to make sure that Molly doesn't see us as we leave. She can't come with us, especially because she's still nursing and we don't even know where we're going. I do think it will be warm, though, since we needed to pack our bathing suits," Scottie said while petting Molly.

Once the girls finished grooming the horses, they took Molly to her pen and lifted out the ramp to make sure she couldn't get out in the morning. Jack said he'd let her out after the girls were out of sight on their horses.

"Boy, am I tired," Sophie yawned after they'd cleaned up and were in their pajamas. "Let's go say goodnight to Ma and Pa so we can finish the next task and get a good night's sleep!"

CHAPTER SIX

Ride to the Tide

Scottie woke up to the rooster crowing just as the sun began to rise. She wasn't sure what was in store for her and Sophie, but she did know from Auntie Jill's instructions that wherever their magical frame was going to take them, they were going to ride their horses through it!

"Come on, Sophie, wake up!" Scottie ordered as she threw her pillow at Sophie.

"Okay, okay," Sophie yawned.

"The backpacks are ready to go, we got a good night's sleep, and now we need to put the frame in one of our packs," Sophie said after returning to their room from eating breakfast.

"Since you packed the rain box, I'll pack the frame," Scottie said, making room in her backpack for it. "Remember when we first got the frame from Auntie Jill and I thought it was boring?"

"I sure do. You were so disappointed until it began to change all sorts of colors," Sophie remembered. "And then when it grew as big as our bedroom with that parrot flying in, we were in shock and didn't know what to do," she continued with a laugh.

"Yep, and little did we know that the parrot was Dr. Drake's and it was named Papaya," Scottie added. "That reminds me. I wonder where Papaya was while Dr. Drake and Auntie Jill were getting married."

"I asked him at the wedding where she was and he said that Papaya was waiting for us in a different location!"

"What does he mean 'waiting for us'?" Scottie asked but not waiting for an answer. "I'll bet he was hinting about our next adventure!" she announced.

"You may be right. I didn't think much about it but that's probably what Dr. Drake was referring to," Sophie said thoughtfully.

"You know, sis, because Dr. Drake is so worldly and knowledgeable, I don't feel comfortable calling him Uncle Rusty," Sophie decided.

"I don't either. It just doesn't sound right. I know, let's call him Uncle Drake instead!"

"Great idea, Scottie. From now on, he's Uncle Drake to us!" Sophie exclaimed. "Oh, I almost forgot to put Maptrixter in my backpack!" (It was up to Sophie to be the keeper of Maptrixter when Dr. Drake told her the map was now hers.)

Once that was decided, the girls put on their cowboy boots, a light jacket, and picked up their backpacks to head for the kitchen to say goodbye to Ma and Pa, who were still drinking their morning coffee.

"What a beautiful morning, girls," Pa said while reading the morning paper and sipping a hot cup of coffee. "You two sure are up early this morning."

"We wanted to get an early start for our new adventure, I mean, horse ride today," Scottie said without giving too much away about their plans on the ranch.

"Ma tells me that you two are pretending to go to a faraway land and then you want to camp out in the courtyard under the stars," Pa commented while looking at Ma and then their backpacks.

"If that's okay with you, Pa," Sophie replied.

"That sounds like a very summery thing to do," Pa said with a smile as he stood up to pour himself another cup.

"Oh, good," both girls sighed.

"Have a great ride girls, but remember, home by supper," Ma said as she gave each girl a hug and a kiss.

Sophie and Scottie hugged Ma a little longer than usual, knowing that they wouldn't see her for a few days (in frame time, of course).

"Whew, I didn't think we'd get on this trail so early this morning," Sophie said as she steered Firefly onto the Oak Branch Trail. "I am so curious about what's in the third envelope."

"The envelope!" Scottie blurted out.

"Don't worry. I put it in the outer pocket of my backpack," Sophie said calmly as she patted her pack behind her.

"So according to the next instruction, we can open the third envelope after we turn right at Bear Rock, which Maptrixter showed us," Scottie reviewed out loud. "Is that right?"

"Yep, that's right," Sophie agreed as they rode along the trail.

Soon the two were at Bear Rock and turned onto the trail that passes it. After riding a little while, Sophie could tell that Starburst was ready to gallop.

"I think you should open the third envelope now, Sophie," Scottie suggested. "Starburst wants to gallop along this flat part of the trail, but I think we should open it up."

"Okay, sis," Sophie said as she reached for the third envelope, steering Firefly to walk next to Scottie so they both could see what Sophie pulled out of the envelope.

Both girls held their breath as Sophie pulled out a photograph. On the back of it was a note from Auntie Jill.

Dear Sophie and Scottie,
Congratulations, you are now ready to begin another amazing journey. Sophie, I need you to put your rain box in the outer pocket of your backpack with the lid off of it. Scottie, I need you to get off of Starburst, give the reins to Sophie to hold, and put the picture in the frame. Then I want you to walk 20 big steps down the trail from where the horses are right now and set the frame with the picture

in it on the ground in the center of the trail with the picture toward you and the horses. Once you do this, I need you to find the rock next to where Firefly and Sophie are waiting. Use the rock to get back onto Starburst. After that, you will know what to do next.

Have a great ride!

Love,

Auntie Jill and Uncle Drake

Quickly, both Scottie and Sophie looked around and sure enough, there was a rock for Scottie to climb on so she could easily get back onto Starburst!

"Well, this must be the place on the trail because there is the rock," Scottie said with a nervous laugh. "And how did Auntie Jill know we were going to call Dr. Drake, Uncle Drake?"

"I don't know, but let's get going before I change my mind and go back home," Sophie said, looking back on the trail toward the direction of the ranch house.

"Okay, okay, I've got the frame so give me the photo. I haven't really looked at what is in the picture at all," Scottie said while turning it over. "Oh, wow, Sophie, this place looks amazing."

In the picture was an enormous mountain with lots of green grass in the lower portion. Up the mountain, the grass turned to shrubs and trees, almost like a jungle. A trail in the lower grassy area was perfect for the horses to walk on. The sky was blue, with a few clouds at the top of the mountain.

75

"I guess we'll be riding on that trail," Scottie said as she put the picture in the frame. "Okay, I'll be back in a few minutes." She looked at the picture, and the frame began to sparkle and turn lots of colors as she counted 20 big steps.

When Scottie had done what the instructions stated, she jogged back, climbed onto the rock, and then sat on Starburst, who was getting very restless and was ready to go.

"Whoa, Starburst, we'll get going pretty soon," Scottie soothed while petting Starburst's neck. "The frame was still really colorful as I set it down on the ground."

Both girls looked down the trail at the frame. It looked so small on the open trail. Then suddenly, as if the frame was tired of showing its colors, it just stopped!

"There look," Scott shouted at Sophie, "the frame is growing bigger than it did in our room!"

Soon the frame with the picture in it was so large that the girls couldn't see over it or around it! In fact, Sophie noticed a warm breeze coming from the picture. Scottie started to sniff the air and could smell what seemed like a slight salty scent. Suddenly, both girls heard a "whoosh" sound, as if a pail of water was being splashed against the side of a house! They could see a large spray of water about 15 feet high going up, which blocked the view of the mountain and then crashed down on something, sending the water onto the trail as well.

As the girls observed this, Scottie pointed to something flying right toward them and landing about five feet away on the trail.

"Oh, my!" Sophie stated. "That is a seagull and it just landed on our trail!"

"Look out!" Scottie shouted as another seagull flew over their heads with a fish in its beak. The bird lost its grip of the fish and it dropped, almost hitting Starburst between the ears. Just before it landed, the other seagull standing on the trail used its powerful wings to lift itself up and caught the fish in mid-air!

"Well, that was close," Scottie said. She brushed some dirt that came off the seagull's webbed feet and landed onto Starburst's bangs, or forelock, between her eyes.

"Where do you think the water is coming from?" Scottie asked Sophie.

"From what I can see and smell, I'd say that the water was a wave crashing on some rocks that aren't in the picture," Sophie began to answer. "So from where we are standing, we are over the ocean!"

"Wow, this is amazing," Scottie said, staring at the scenery in front of her. She then realized that they'd better do something. "I guess we'd better get going after the next wave crashes in front of us or the frame will begin to shrink again."

"I don't know if I can do this. Firefly doesn't like water." Sophie hesitated while waiting for the next wave to come.

"I know. Starburst keeps pulling on the reins with her mouth, ready to go. So just as I begin to gallop her toward the mountain, have Firefly right behind me. She'll be so concerned about being behind Starburst that she won't even notice any water, or ocean, or wherever the water is coming from," Scottie suggested.

"Alright, that sounds like a good plan," Sophie agreed and both girls began to walk the horses toward the ranch house to get more galloping room.

Once the horses were turned back toward the mountain, Scottie yelled out, "Hayah!"

Instantly, Starburst leaped forward as if she were in a rodeo relay to go around some barrels. As soon as Firefly saw her take off, she began to gallop too. The horses and riders got closer and closer to the trail in the giant picture. It was only a matter of time before the next wave would hit the land.

"Come on! Come on!" Scottie shouted as the horses were almost there.

Starburst crossed over onto the new trail first, with Firefly right behind her. Just as she did this, a new wave came crashing against the rocks and got the back of Firefly's legs and tail wet. This startled her so much that she jumped forward as if to clear a fence, which almost made Sophie fall off.

"Whoa, girl!" Sophie yelled while trying to steady her on the grassy trail.

Each girl stopped and turned her horse around. They saw a vast coastline and an ocean glistening from the sun's rays as far as their eyes could see.

"This is beautiful," they said breathlessly. Their ranch was nowhere in sight. Sophie noticed a tugging feeling in the outer pocket of her backpack, as if something was put into it. She decided that she'd look into the pocket later.

In the distance they heard some pounding steps coming toward them. A man waving his hat over his head and holding the horse reins in the other was approaching.

The girls looked at each other and looked at the man and yelled, "Uncle Drake!"

As he got close enough for them to hear him, he shouted, "Welcome, welcome to Amelia Island!"

The girls rode up to Uncle Drake with big smiles on their faces. Sophie saw something out of the corner of her eye and looked quickly toward that image. It was Papaya flying in fast from the ocean breeze that she had caught in flight. She buzzed Sophie's hair and then landed on Uncle Drake's shoulder.

"I'm so glad you girls decided it was time for another journey. We here on the island could really use your help," Uncle Drake stated as he reached over and hugged each niece while sitting on his horse.

Just as he said that, Sophie and Scottie noticed another rider coming toward them.

"Auntie Jill!" Scottie shouted as she joined them.

"My two favorite nieces!" their auntie announced. She stopped her horse and also leaned over to give each girl a hug. "Your uncle and I were just saying last night that it would be perfect if you two decided to ride through the frame soon for another adventure."

"How long have you and Uncle Drake been here on the island?" Sophie asked while pulling back on Firefly's reins to keep her standing still.

"We got here right after the wedding, but I need to leave first thing in the morning for another project. I'm glad that I didn't miss you two," Auntie Jill replied with a smile.

"Alright you three, we could be here all day chit-chatting about one thing or another," Uncle Drake teased as he looked at the girls and then to Auntie Jill. "Let's ride over to the stables and show the girls where the horses will be kept and also where they will be staying on this cattle ranch."

"There are cattle on this island?" Sophie asked as she looked around for the steers.

"Yep, and so much more. You see, this island is a research center in the middle of the Pacific Ocean," Uncle Drake replied. "We'll fill you in once we get to your yurt."

"What's a yurt?" Scottie asked.

"You'll see. Follow us," Uncle Drake said and made a clicking noise with his mouth. His horse along with the others began to trot and soon lope on the trail toward the ranch with the mountain almost watching them.

The girls could see the cattle grazing in the upper slopes of the grassy areas at the foot of the mountain. Sophie and Scottie could also see a large building with huge bamboo posts holding up a roof covered in thick and long grasses. It was a little farther down the pathway as they reached the horse stables.

"This is where you will keep your horses. The stand over there is where your saddle and bridle will be kept. The box next to the stand is where the brushes are stored for when you need to brush the horses. Now, let's take you to your yurt."

After the horses were settled into their new stables, both girls barely watched where they were going on the pathway as they were constantly looking around

80

as they walked. The plants next to the trail were lush and green with beautiful flowers. Sophie took a deep breath and could smell their sweet tropical scent.

"What kind of flowering tree is that?" Sophie asked, pointing to the huge tree that was covered in small, five-pedal yellow flowers.

"That is called a plumeria tree and the island is covered with them," Auntie Jill explained. "They also bloom in white with yellow, in pink with red stripes on the back of the pedals, and in other colors. Each has a different smell. Now, here we are, your sleeping quarters for as long as you are on the island."

"Wow, this is neat!" Scottie exclaimed as she walked up the five steps leading to the front porch door.

"What kind of building is this?" Sophie asked while touching the walls made of a material that reminded her of a sail on a sailboat or a heavy-duty tent.

"This 'ger,' or home, is called a yurt, a structure that has been used extensively by the Mongolians as well as people in other parts of Central Asia," Uncle Drake explained. "The oldest known yurt used as a home was back in Greece at around 484 BC. So we know that they are sturdy and are perfect for shelter on the island."

The yurt was round with a 15-foot diameter. It had the one door and a window on each side of it. Once Uncle Drake opened the door of the round structure, they all walked in. The girls noticed another window on the back side of the yurt.

"Okay, girls, there are bunk beds over there. You two will have to decide who gets the upper bunk," Auntie Jill said with a smile. "The dresser has two drawers in it to put your things in, and the bathroom is behind that door over there. It's simple, but I think these yurts are actually kind of cute and they work really well."

"So, what do you two think of your yurt?" Uncle Drake asked. He held his arms out to emphasize the room after he and Auntie Jill showed the girls their island home.

The walls and ceiling of cloth were held up with wooden boards about one foot apart. In between the wall boards were other boards that crisscrossed over one another in a lattice pattern to strengthen the boards and walls even more. The ceiling boards went from the top of the wall to the highest point of the ceiling, all meeting together at the center about 15 feet above the ground. All of the ceiling wood boards and wall lattice boards were covered on the outside of the yurt with a layer of felt and then a layer of thick cotton canvas material.

"We love it!" the girls blurted out at the same time and they ran up to hug him and their auntie.

"Good. The canvas walls are really sturdy. Just keep the door closed so the island critters and the rain don't get in," Uncle Drake said with a wink. "Now put your things away, get Maptrixter, and meet us at that large building we walked past before we got to your yurt. That is the dining hall. After we eat an early dinner, your aunt and I can use the map to show you where we are on the island."

Auntie Jill and Uncle Drake closed the door behind them as they left, and the girls could see them walk up the path toward their yurt from the back window.

"I get the top bunk," Scottie claimed as she pulled her things out of the backpack. "Look, Sophie, the drawers already have more clothes in them too."

"Uncle Drake and Auntie Jill sure take care of us," Sophie remarked as she unpacked her things. "Let's hurry because I'm hungry."

Sophie made sure to get Maptrixter, and soon both girls were walking up the steps to the dining hall where Uncle Drake and Auntie Jill were waiting for them. The food was buffet style, where they got a tray and a plate and went to the food stations that appealed to each one. As soon as everyone had what they wanted, they sat down at a large round table. As the sun became lower in the sky, other islanders came to eat in the cafeteria. Uncle Drake and Auntie Jill introduced the girls to anyone who asked them who they were. Sophie noticed that most were students, professors, or doctors like Uncle Drake.

"What is this island used for?" Sophie asked.

"This is a research island and is part of the Pacific Remote Islands. What that means is that we are about half way between Hawaii and Australia," Uncle Drake continued. "We call this Amelia Island for..."

"Amelia Earhart!" Scottie announced.

"Why, yes, you've heard of her?" Auntie Jill asked in an amused tone.

"We learned about her when we had to do a report on women aviators," Scottie replied. "I learned that she was the first female aviator to fly across the Atlantic Ocean by herself. I also learned that while she was trying to fly around the world, her plane mysteriously disappeared over the Pacific Ocean in 1937."

"That's right. She was thought to have landed her plane on a remote island called Nikumaroro Island while trying to find the larger Howland Island. That island is part of the Coral Islands not far from this one. So to honor her, we named this land Amelia Island," Auntie Jill explained. "In fact, some islanders have claimed to have seen her on parts of this island. Just folklore, I'm sure. Now, is everyone done eating?"

The girls nodded and began to clear the table where they ate. After the table was clear and just the four of them were sitting there, Sophie took off the rubber band that was around Maptrixter and carefully unrolled it onto the table.

CHAPTER SEVEN

Amelia Island

The girls were amazed at how detailed the map showed everything. They could see where the ranch was on the island and noticed the moving cattle grazing below the mountain! In fact, they could hear the waves crashing up against the cliffs on another part of the island as well.

"Look how Maptrixter has changed into Amelia Island," Sophie observed. "I can't wait to explore everything!"

"Now, hold on you two," Uncle Drake began. "There are parts of the island we don't even know about, so don't think you can get on your horses and just ride wherever you want to go. In fact, there is work to be done on the ranch and then I will show you around the island myself."

"Should we be focusing somewhere on Trixter once our work is done?" Scottie asked.

"There are some unexplained, uh, phenomena that have been happening here on the island that I will tell you about later," Uncle Drake replied, "but first we want to show you two one of the most amazing sunsets you'll ever see."

Uncle Drake got up from the table as Sophie rolled Maptrixter back up and secured it with the rubber band. The girls looked at each other with excitement as they walked out of the dining hall and followed Uncle Drake and Auntie Jill to the other side of the building. About 50 yards from where they stood was a gazebo that overlooked a cliff above the vast ocean beyond the island. As they reached the gazebo, the sun was almost touching the ocean horizon. The white water of the waves was washed in a golden light as it curled over onto the blue water below it. The girls were silent while watching such beauty. Even Dr. Drake and Auntie Jill were amazed at the splendor of the setting sun as it went down into the horizon.

"The sunsets on this island never get old," Uncle Drake said as they stood up to walk back to their yurt. "You'll need to get a good night's sleep, girls. We have some cattle to round up in the morning! I'll have Papaya fly over to your window just after sunrise to wake you up. If you need anything, remember our yurt is just down the trail from yours." Uncle Drake pointed down the path and the girls could easily see where they were staying.

"So you won't be joining us tomorrow morning, Auntie Jill?" Sophie asked.

"No, your Uncle Drake will be with you for the entire time you are on the island. Remember, I told you that I have another project that needs my attention? But you, my dears," Auntie Jill continued looking from Sophie to Scottie, "are needed here on the island."

She kissed each girl on the forehead and Uncle Drake hugged them saying, "Goodnight you two. I will see you first thing in the morning."

Papaya had just landed on his shoulder and let out a squawk as if to say goodnight as well, which made the girls giggle.

"This is really neat. I've never seen a sunset like that before," Scottie said as she walked into the yurt, "and I've never slept in a round hut before. I like it!"

"I like it too. I wonder how the horses will react to the cattle. I mean, we have mostly sheep back at our ranch," Sophie said while getting ready for bed.

"I'm sure they will be fine," Scottie replied with toothpaste in her mouth. "Just keep Firefly behind Starburst on the trails and she'll stay calm."

"I guess you're right," Sophie agreed and then yawned. "Hurry and climb up the ladder to the top bunk. I'm tired and want to go to sleep."

As soon as Sophie said that, both girls heard a rattling noise from the outer pocket of Sophie's backpack. Quickly, Sophie got out of bed and realized that she had forgotten to check her outer pocket when she unpacked her things.

"Oh my, look Scottie," Sophie said while taking out her rain box and pulling off the lid. "We have a stowaway. It's the frame!"

The rain box wasn't very large. It was about a three-inch square covered in red leather with a beautiful pattern of many colored beads on the lid. Each girl had received one as a gift from Auntie Jill.

"How can the frame fit in there? It's three times the size of that box," Scottie exclaimed.

"I don't know. It shrunk, I guess, because there it is and without the photo of the island in it," Sophie observed as she pulled the frame out of the rain box. "I think I'll put it back in the box for safekeeping. We just don't know what the frame will do if left by itself on that dresser over there."

"Good idea, sis, but also put the box in your drawer so it will be out of sight. I'm so tired. Let's get some shut-eye before I'm too tired to climb up the ladder to go to bed," Scottie said while rubbing her eyes.

"Goodnight, Scottie. Say a prayer for Ma and Pa and Molly," Sophie said as she turned out the light.

The sunlight was soon shining on Amelia Island and very brightly into Sophie and Scottie's yurt. Just as Uncle Drake said, Papaya was at their window squawking and squawking until Scottie told her they were awake and would get ready for their horse ride. Scottie also noticed something other than fruit in her beak and opened the window screen to pull it from her. It was a note from Uncle Drake saying that he would meet them for breakfast at half past the hour. Then they'd go to the stables to saddle up the horses.

"Sophie, wake up," Scottie ordered, pushing her a little on her shoulder. "We need to meet Uncle Drake so WAKE UP!"

"Okay, okay," Sophie replied as she got out of her bed. "This is going to be quite an adventure-filled day, so I'll be sure to bring Maptrixter with me. I'll tie it to my saddle in case we get separated from Uncle Drake while rounding up the cattle."

After breakfast, the girls and Uncle Drake were on their horses and heading out toward the trails they were on yesterday after riding through the frame.

"I'm sure you girls have noticed how long the grass is over on that hillside about a mile from here," Uncle Drake said while pointing to the part of the lower mountain they were riding toward. "These grasslands are very fertile due to the mountain soil. This used to be a volcano, which is now dormant, and because the dirt is very rich with nutrients, the grass grows fast and thick. Those upper grasslands are where we are going to bring the cattle to graze."

Dr. Drake, Sophie, and Scottie joined other ranchers on their horses and were a part of the cattle drive from one grassland to the more lush area. Scottie and Starburst were ready for the challenge and began to get behind the 50 head of cattle to encourage them to quit grazing and head for the upper grasslands. Sophie noticed that this lower area was very close to the cliffs where the waves crashed up against them. As she observed the cliffs, she spotted someone running down a very narrow trail, which became hidden from sight because of the thick plumeria trees and other tropical shrubs.

"Hmm, I wonder where she is going. I'll have to check Maptrixter to see if this trail shows up on it," Sophie thought to herself. She then quickly noticed that Scottie and the others were quite a ways away from her and Firefly, so she began to gallop to catch up to them.

The cattle were, for the most part, cooperating and going the way the ranchers wanted them to go. Scottie noticed a smaller steer was rebelling and starting to trot up a trail a little farther away from the other steers. Being the "expert" cattle rustler she had now become, she decided to gallop Starburst toward the animal, run ahead to get in front of it, and turn the steer back to the other cattle. Then, suddenly, a loud snap in the upper bushes spooked Starburst!

"Whoa, whoa!" Scottie shouted but it was no use. Starburst was in what is known as a dead run and wasn't going to stop until the trail ended. All Scottie could do was crouch up onto the horse's shoulders and lower neck area and hold on to her thick black mane. Tears were streaming from the outer corners of Scottie's eyes as Starburst continued to race up the trail. As the two were speeding up the mountain, the trail finally stopped and so did Starburst. In fact, the horse stopped so quickly that Scottie sailed right over her head onto a dry and sandy river bed ahead of them.

"Wow, Starburst," Scottie blurted out as she stood up and brushed herself off. "I never knew you could run so fast!"

Starburst walked up to Scottie, still breathing heavily and nudged her almost as if she was apologizing to Scottie. Scottie petted her face and looked around where she had landed. She noticed some silver threads of material in the river bed, thinking how pretty it was. Scottie checked each horse leg to make sure Starburst wasn't hurt. As Scottie lifted each leg to check her hooves, she noticed something odd. Each horseshoe was a little loose. It was as if the nails in the iron shoe were slightly pulled out.

"Scottie, Scottie, are you okay?" Sophie cried out as she came trotting up the path, trying to find her sister.

"I'm fine, just a little shaken and dirty," Scottie called back to her as Sophie came into view. "Did you see how fast Starburst was running? You'd think she was a race horse!"

"I know. I looked up and saw her running up this trail so fast. I knew I wouldn't be able to catch up until now. I told Uncle Drake that I'd come and see if everything was okay. He'll probably ride up here if we don't go back down the hill soon."

"You should get off of Firefly and check her shoes. All of Starburst's shoes are a little loose," Scottie suggested.

Sophie got off of her horse and checked each hoof. Sure enough, they were all slightly loose.

"That's weird. I don't know why their horseshoes wouldn't be secure. They just got new ones last week."

"I know, very strange. Hey, Sophie, I wonder where this trail over here goes to?" Scottie asked. She looked around to see if the ground was extra hard or rocky, which might explain why the nails had been pulled out.

Scottie had walked about 10 steps before she came to some thick vines that were in a kind of circle. As she pulled the shrubs apart, she found a small round hut, almost like a yurt but the walls were hard like cement. Suddenly, as Scottie got closer to the building, her body jerked forward as if something was pulling her. She was able to pull back with some effort and realized that her belt buckle was pulling away from her body and toward the hut!

"Come over here, Sophie. Look what my belt buckle is doing. It's as if it's attracted to this hut. In fact, I wonder what this hut is doing here in the middle of the island."

Sophie walked over after tying up Firefly next to Starburst. She looked at Scottie's belt buckle and pulled it away from the hut, feeling the tension between the buckle and the building. She then began to walk more around the structure and found a door with a giant padlock on it.

"I don't know what this hut is for, but whatever is in it, the owner doesn't want anyone to know," Sophie observed while pulling on the lock and trying to open it.

"Sophie, Scottie, where are you?"

The girls looked at each other in that knowing way as if to say that they may need to come back later. With a little more effort, Scottie pulled her buckle away from the building and she turned and followed Sophie back to the horses.

"We're over here, Uncle Drake," Scottie shouted as she and Sophie untied their horses' reins from the branch of a rubber tree next to the trail.

Riding up to them, Uncle Drake shouted, "Is everyone okay?"

"Oh, I'm all right, just a few scrapes from flying over Starburst's head when she suddenly stopped," Scottie answered with a slight smile and rubbed her elbow.

"I'm a little sore but I'm fine. We might need to check all of the horses' shoes to make sure they aren't loose because Starburst's and Firefly's shoes are."

"Hmm, that is odd but most of the horses here don't have horseshoes because the trails are rather soft. We'll make sure they get fixed, but it may be a day before you two can ride again," Uncle Drake replied.

The girls nodded and started down the trail toward the stables. Once there, Sophie made sure that she took Maptrixter from her saddle, and they all returned to their yurts to get cleaned up for an early dinner.

"I can't stop thinking about that strange concrete hut up above the upper grassland of the mountain," Scottie said while changing into clean clothes. "It's as if the building had a strange pull on my belt buckle."

"I think I figured out what was happening," Sophie said as she brushed her hair. "I think there is some sort of magnetic force field around that hut and on the trail, which would explain why the horses' shoes became loose. It also makes sense why the island ranchers aren't aware of this force because their horses don't have shoes."

"I think you're on to something, Sophie," Scottie agreed.

"I was hoping we'd be able to ride tomorrow," Sophie said. As she and Scottie left their yurt to walk to the dining hall, Sophie continued, "I want to show you something I noticed earlier today on the lower trail, but first we need to look on Maptrixter too."

"Ooh, a mystery. I'm all eyes and ears, sis," Scottie whispered as they waved to Uncle Drake and walked into the dining hall.

"Hi, girls. I wanted to let you know that the ranch workers were very impressed with the way you two helped move the cattle to the upper grasslands," Uncle Drake said while they stood in line to get their dinner. "They were also glad that you didn't get hurt after Starburst got spooked and ran up that trail. In fact, Kimo, the ranch manager, said no one ever goes on that trail anymore since the last earthquake, which split the trail into a ravine and then it went back together again. That is why the overgrown path is called Earthquake Trail."

"An earthquake?" the girls asked in rather concerned voices.

"Yes, but don't worry," Uncle Drake said in a calming tone with a smile. "That happened a very long time ago. There are still quakes on the island, but not as big as that one. It isn't unusual to have an earthquake on these Pacific islands, but they are rarely large enough to endanger anyone. The huge mountain that Earthquake Trail is on used to be an active volcano. In fact, the islanders now call it the Sleeping Giant."

Both girls let out a sigh of relief and followed Uncle Drake to an open table. Once they had all eaten, Kimo told them that the horses' shoes would be fixed tomorrow and they could ride in the afternoon if they wanted to.

"Be sure to stay on the well-marked dirt roads and no more racing up Earthquake Trail," Kimo said with a chuckle before he left them to eat the ice cream that Uncle Drake had gotten for them.

"Don't worry. I won't be riding on that trail again!" Scottie replied convincingly.

"Since we can't ride until later in the day," their uncle began, "how would you girls like to try some snorkeling in the lagoon to the west of here? The water there is warm and very clear. The only recent changes are the currents and tides of the island, so we'll swim in the lagoon not too far from shore. The oceanographers on the island are keeping a close watch on these changes."

"We'd love to snorkel, but we might need a few lessons," Sophie answered.

"What is an oceanog...what you said," Scottie asked.

"An oceanographer is a person who studies the oceans and everything in it," Uncle Drake replied. "In fact, that is what the people on this island are all about, studying the island, its waters, and how plants and animals grow here. Once you girls see how beautiful and clear the water is here surrounding the island, I was hoping you could help us solve this ocean current and tide mystery we seem to be having."

"We would love to help!" both girls announced with excitement.

"Good. Now you two should go check on Starburst and Firefly before you head back to your yurt for the night," Uncle Drake suggested while petting Papaya, who had just flown onto his shoulder. "Tomorrow should be a great day for snorkeling."

The girls agreed and were soon walking toward the stables. The students who lived on the island fed the horses alfalfa hay, so the girls didn't have to worry about feeding or giving them water.

"It's weird how we don't have to do much with the horses," Scottie commented as they reached the stables, "so let's at least brush them."

"Good idea," Sophie said as she reached into the large wooden box where the brushes and combs were kept. "Oh my!"

"What is it?" Scottie asked while running over to where Sophie was standing.

Sophie bent over and pulled something out of the box, and it wasn't a brush.

"Now how did you get in here?" Sophie asked in almost a stern tone.

It was Maptrixter! The map was almost pulling Sophie as she carried it toward the closed lid of the other tack box. Sophie took off the rubber band and unrolled the map to see what Maptrixter wanted to show them.

"What is the Trixter up to now?" Scottie asked with her hands on her hips as she looked down on the map.

"I'm not...wait, I think I do know," Sophie said. "See that trail there, the one that is kind of glowing, that is where I was looking around and noticed a woman running into that grove of plumeria trees and bushes. She had short hair, almost how our great grandma used to wear hers in the 1940s. She stopped and looked back at me and then she was gone under the trees."

"Wow, sis, that is strange," Scottie agreed, looking at where the trail was in regard to where they were in the stables. "You know, we really aren't that far from that trail. I mean, we have our hiking shoes on and I

96

bet we could walk to that trail, look into those trees, and get back before the sun sets."

"I don't know, Scottie," Sophie said hesitantly. "I don't want to get lost or into any trouble."

"We won't get into any trouble. We have Maptrixter to show us the way and, look, we have company."

Just as Scottie said that, Papaya flew in and perched herself on one of the rubber tree branches near where they stood. So after they were done brushing their horses, Scottie and Sophie headed for the glowing trail, with Papaya flying near them and Maptrixter securely held in Sophie's right hand.

CHAPTER EIGHT

Oceanic Institute 8.6

As the girls walked on the trail, they noticed beautiful flowering plants, large trees, and many different types of colorful birds. Soon they were at the edge of the plumeria tree grove.

"Let me unroll Maptrixter and see if it suggests what we do next," Sophie said. "Look, here we are, and the trail continues to glow all the way through the trees. It stops at this large mossy boulder."

"Then what are we waiting for? Let's go!" Scottie said excitedly.

"I don't know, Scottie. I feel that we should go back and get Uncle Drake."

"If we do that, then the sun will be setting and who knows if Maptrixter will show us any more of the trail," Scottie replied. "Besides, don't you want to see where that mysterious lady went?"

"I guess so. Okay, let's go," Sophie said while rolling up Maptrixter.

Soon the girls (with Papaya flying overhead) were walking underneath hundreds of fragrant plumeria branches. Each tree seemed to touch the branch of the other tree, as the girls looked up at the beautiful flowers on the tree branches.

"This is so pretty. Ma would love this," Sophie said in almost a whisper.

The end of the trail led them to a mossy boulder that was very rough to touch. As Scottie leaned on it with one hand to take a sticker out of her sock, the boulder began to move very slowly and steadily while making a grinding sound until it came to a halt, revealing another trail!

"Oh wow, sis, this must be why the trail was glowing. We would have never known to walk here if Trixter hadn't shown us!" Scottie proclaimed.

"I can't believe that this huge boulder, which I believe is made of volcanic rock, just moved!" Sophie said with very wide eyes. "Papaya, you stay out here. If we don't come back soon, go get Uncle Drake."

Papaya seemed to know exactly what Sophie ordered and perched herself on one of the plumeria branches.

With Maptrixter in hand, the girls began to walk into a sort of cave, more like a tube, a lava tube. There were holes above them here and there that let the sunlight into the tube so the girls could easily see where they were going. As they walked for about 5 minutes, the tube began to fill with more light. The girls could hear a sort of swishing sound as they got closer to the lit part of the tube.

"What is this place?" Sophie whispered to Scottie. "I've never seen anything like this before."

"I'm not sure, but I don't think we should walk under it," Scottie replied in the same whisper.

As the girls took two steps into this part of the tube, they looked up and all around them. They couldn't believe their eyes. The rock lava tube had now transformed into a glass-like tube. They could see the long strands of seaweed that were attached on the ocean floor swaying back and forth against the clear tube walls. Schools of silvery colored fish were dashing one way and then another above them, making glittery patterns in the water. Large bunches of colorful coral were spread out from the tube as far as the eye could see. Every type of colorful tropical fish imaginable was foraging among the multicolored coral for food. A shadow was cast over their heads, which made them look up to see a very large creature gliding over them. Both girls caught their breath as the huge fish swam out of view.

"I don't think we should go any farther," Sophie said hesitantly.

"I don't think we should either," Scottie agreed. "I can see that we could walk quite a ways out into the ocean. I mean look how dry the sandy trail is. Well, maybe a few more steps."

Suddenly, the water current began to violently flow back and forth, back and forth against the clear tube walls. The girls could feel the earth beneath them begin to move and a loud roar filled the tube!

"Hurry, Scottie. We have to get out of here. I think it's an earthquake!" Sophie yelled as she pulled Scottie's arm and they began to run back to the entrance of the lava tube. A few pieces of the rock wall came loose and fell to the ground as the girls ran through the entrance. And then, as quickly as it began, the shaking stopped. Birds were singing and Papaya was still in the tree squawking loudly as if to scold the girls.

Scottie quickly turned around after spotting Papaya and heard a loud crash, as if two rocks had hit against one another. "Darn, the boulder slipped back into place," she said in disappointment.

"I think that is best. Walking into that tube was a dumb thing to do," Sophie said in a scolding tone. "I don't care if we ever see this place or that mysterious woman again!"

"You're right. That was crazy what we just did," Scottie replied. "We better not tell Uncle Drake. I think it will make him pretty mad at us."

"I don't like to keep things from him, but in this case, I think you're right," Sophie said as she looked around for Maptrixter. "Oh no! I think I dropped the map when I panicked and pulled your arm to run out of the lava tube."

"What?!" Scottie instantly turned toward the boulders and began to hit it with her fist, hoping that the giant rock would slide open as it did before. But nothing happened. "Just great, now what are we going to do?" Scottie asked in an irritated tone of voice.

"We'll have to come back I guess, but not now," Sophie answered. "I'll just tell Uncle Drake that I left it in the yurt if he asks me where Maptrixter is." The girls quickly walked on the trail back to the stables, where Uncle Drake was waiting for them.

"I looked around the stables to make sure the horses were okay and realized that you two weren't here," Uncle Drake observed. "Where were you?

"Oh, after we had brushed the horses, we decided to walk around a little bit on the dirt road and go see the water. But then we realized that it was too far of a walk," Sophie explained.

"Papaya joined us too," Scottie added. "Um, Uncle Drake, did you feel the earthquake?"

"Why, no I didn't, but I did learn about it from the people at Oceanic Institute 8.6. It was a small temblor, as we like to call it, just outside the lagoon on the ocean floor," he answered. "I'm surprised you two could feel it walking on the dirt road. You must be sensitive to the ground moving."

"That's probably it," Scottie agreed. "It scared us at first, but when we saw that Papaya wasn't bothered, we weren't worried any more either."

Sophie nodded as Scottie was talking, and both followed Uncle Drake as he began to walk back to the yurts, pointing out different kinds of plants on the way.

"There is a mini refrigerator with fruits and other snacks that I had delivered to your yurt so you can eat something before you go to bed. I know we had an early dinner, and you two might be hungry," Uncle Drake told them while they were walking. "I'll have Papaya wake you up again just after sunrise so we will be swimming in the lagoon when it is really calm."

"That sounds great," Sophie agreed, "but what is Oceanic Institute 8.6?"

"Oh, I'll tell you all about it tomorrow. OI86 is the reason we're all here on this island," Uncle Drake said with a smile. "Now here is your yurt, so goodnight and don't stay up too late. Oh, and don't worry about Maptrixter. The map is safest to stay where it is."

Both girls didn't know what to say to Uncle Drake as they waved goodnight to him.

"What did he mean by saying Maptrixter is safe where it is?" Scottie asked in a surprised tone.

"I think he meant that it is best to keep the map in our yurt for now. It could get wet or something if we take it snorkeling with us." Sophie, feeling worried as she answered, hoped Maptrixter was fine and not in danger.

"I'm wondering what OI86 wants with us and what the institute does anyway," Scottie said while looking into the fridge. "Oh yum, there are some cut-up mangos in here and it looks like pretzels dipped in chocolate. Do you want any, sis?"

"An institute usually performs studies of some kind, so maybe they want to see our reaction to something. Who knows? But I can't wait for tomorrow to come," Sophie excitedly replied. "Pass me some of those mangos before you eat them all!"

"Okay, okay."

"I just realized that I haven't checked on my rain box in a while," Sophie said with a mouthful of mangoes and opened up her dresser drawer. "It looks fine and the frame is still in it."

"That's good," Scottie yawned.

After the girls had their fill of snacks and got ready for bed, Sophie couldn't stop thinking about Maptrixter and the mysterious woman she had seen on the trail. What if she finds the map? Or what if the map gets ruined by a crab that wants it for its home? Sophie shook her head as if to get these thoughts out of her mind and then was fast asleep.

Papaya had to squawk a little bit longer to wake the girls up in the morning, but they were up quickly and ready for their first lagoon adventure. They were familiar with snorkeling, as Pa had bought them each a snorkel, mask, and fins to swim in the pond on the ranch. But this would be different and the girls were really looking forward to it. After breakfast, Dr. Drake picked them up in an all-terrain vehicle, or ATV, that didn't have a top on it.

"Are you girls ready to go?" Uncle Drake asked as he made room for their backpacks filled with towels, sun block, and snacks.

"We sure are!"

"How far are we from the lagoon?" Scottie asked as she put on her safety belt.

"We are about 20 minutes from the perfect snorkeling spot. We'll see all sorts of colorful sea life and corals," Uncle Drake replied with a smile, "so buckle up and let's go!"

The dirt road was a little bouncy in the ATV, but the girls laughed at every bounce and jerky motion that they felt. The road took them right past the trail that Maptrixter showed the girls toward the lava tube. Sophie blinked a couple of times and couldn't believe what she was seeing. The mysterious woman was standing and watching them just inside the shaded area of the plumeria trees. It looked like she was holding something that was rolled up in her hand.

"Oh my!" Sophie blurted out loud.

"What, sis?" Scottie asked as the ATV was out of the woman's sight.

"Oh, nothing. I'll tell you later," Sophie answered as she turned her head back to try to get a glimpse of the woman.

Twenty minutes went by quickly and soon the ATV stopped on a beach with miles and miles of sand. The water was a beautiful teal blue and as smooth as glass. This was going to be fun. Even Uncle Drake was taking everything out of the ATV as quickly as possible so they could get into the lagoon.

"Now, girls, here are your masks, fins, and snorkels," he explained. "Have you two ever snorkeled before?"

"Yes, we have," Scottie answered for them both, "in our pond."

"That's good. This will be the same mechanics of breathing through the mouthpiece and the tube. I want you girls to use these life vests too. This way you can just float around without getting too tired," Uncle Drake explained.

The girls agreed and soon were walking backward into the water because the fins made it too hard to walk forward normally. With their masks now on, all three were entering into another world as they swam in the lagoon. They could see many bright-colored fish, some by themselves and others in schools, all

106

seeming to float with the current from one rock or coral cluster to another, pecking at the object to find food. Many fish swam through colorful coral mini caves and popped out from the other side. Scottie tried to follow one of the fish with a yellow body and a black stripe on its face, but realized that she couldn't go very far underwater with the life vest on. Sophie noticed other fish had blue stripes and some were rainbow colored. All of the fish didn't seem to mind the snorkelers. They were too busy foraging for food on the rocks and the coral. Uncle Drake pointed to a rather tall rock formation, and soon the girls saw several moray eels sticking their heads out slightly from the holes in the rocks that were their home.

"Wow, that was amazing!" Scottie exclaimed as she and Sophie took their fins off to easily walk back to their beach towels.

"I loved all of the sea life under the water," Sophie added as she sat down on her towel. "I could snorkel all day."

"Well, I'm glad you girls enjoyed it. Now let's eat some lunch," Uncle Drake suggested as he pulled out some sandwiches and drinks from the cooler in the ATV.

"Hey, what's that building over there?" Scottie asked and then took a bite of her sandwich.

"Oh, that is Oceanic Institute 8.6, which I mentioned last night," Uncle Drake answered.

"What's the 8.6 stand for, Uncle Drake?" Sophie asked.

"Oceanic Institute 8.6, or OI86 as we all call it, is where all of the ocean studies of this region are performed," he began. "The building you see is just the beginning of a group of buildings that actually go under the surface of the lagoon for 8.6 kilometers and about 30 feet deep."

"That's about 4 miles from the shore line," Sophie said in an amazed voice. "That would almost bring it into the open ocean and out of the lagoon!"

"That's right, Sophie," Uncle Drake agreed. "I'm glad you two are interested in this because the institute will be our next stop. From there, I will teach you girls how to scuba dive!"

"Scuba! That's awesome!" both shouted as they finished their lunch.

"I wanted to see how comfortable you two were while snorkeling, and I'd say you girls are part fish with how easily you took to swimming in the lagoon with all of the fish around you," Uncle Drake remarked as they were walking back to the ATV. "So get your stuff and we'll head for OI86."

Uncle Drake drove the ATV back to the dirt road and soon they were on their way. The 10-minute drive was just as bumpy as their ride to their snorkeling spot. Soon Uncle Drake steered the ATV toward another dirt road with all sorts of trees on either side of it leading to a parking area right next to the pier.

"Okay, girls, we're here. Let's go say hello to the institute's director, Maddie McKenzie. Maddie will show us around and tell us about OI86," Uncle Drake explained as he walked along the pier toward the entrance to the building."

As the girls walked next to him, Scottie noticed an animal floating on its back and then bobbing its head up and down in the water as if watching them while they walked toward the door. She then looked away to see where Uncle Drake was pointing.

"This is the area where I will teach you to scuba dive," Uncle Drake pointed out. "It's a safe area with only a few fish because the bottom is very sandy. If you two feel comfortable after your lesson, then we can get a handful of peas and the fish will swim over to eat right out of your hand."

"That sounds like fun," Sophie said, observing the scuba area.

Scottie looked back into the water to try to see if she could see the animal, but it was gone.

"Hello, hello, welcome to Oceanic Institute 8.6!" a women exclaimed as she was holding out her hand to shake Uncle Drake's hand. "It's so good to see you again, Dr. Drake."

"Sophie, Scottie, this is Maddie McKenzie," Uncle Drake said while shaking her hand. "Miss McKenzie is the director of OI86 and knows everything about it."

"Nice to meet you two, and please, call me Maddie."

Both girls shook her hand and said hello. They noticed that Maddie was tall and very athletic looking, like a swimmer in the Olympics competitions. She had shoulder-length blonde hair that looked a little bit like straw from being in the sun and salty water, and she had kind brown eyes that seemed to be always looking for the next thing to talk about.

"We'd like to have a tour, but first I promised the girls a scuba lesson," Uncle Drake explained.

"Oh, what a treat for you girls," Maddie replied with

a smile. "By all means, that stairway takes you to the dive room where all of the scuba gear is stored. I will watch all of you from the viewing chamber below. You two are going to love it!"

Uncle Drake and the girls found the dive room just as Maddie had said. It had a mini pool in the middle of the room for first-time divers to learn about the equipment and use it properly. The room's walls were of very thick glass, with the room half submerged in the lagoon water. An opening in the far side of the room floor allowed the diver to get into the water easily. Once they were in the lagoon, the girls could see the dive area that Uncle Drake had pointed out when they were walking on the pier.

Scottie walked over to the glass wall to look out toward the water. Suddenly, up popped a wet and furry small animal and it looked right at her with its small round black eyes.

CHAPTER NINE

Bubbles!

"Sophie, quick, come over here!" Scottie ordered as the furry animal was still looking at her. In fact, it began to roll over a few times as if to say "let's play!" Its face looked like a baby teddy bear with a little triangular nose, small round black eyes, and a mouth the same size as its nose. The front finger-like paws of the animal were small like a raccoon's, and it had a long body and wide back webbed feet. It also had a long tail that seemed to help it to balance when it lay on its back floating on the water.

"What is it now, Scottie? You know we need to help Uncle Drake with the equipment so we can get started with our...oh, why, it's an otter!" Sophie said while cutting herself short from scolding Scottie.

"That's what I thought," Scottie said in a knowing tone. "But what is it doing out here in the middle of the Pacific Ocean?"

"That is another one of our mysteries here on the island," Uncle Drake answered. "Maddie can't figure out how he got here, but he's been here for about 6 months now and is like the institute's mascot! In fact, I'll bet he'll join us when we scuba out into the lagoon."

"How fun! I can't wait to get this lesson started," Scottie announced.

The girls still had their swimsuits on under their shorts and t-shirts (which were getting pretty dirty from the dust of the ATV ride.) They took their outer clothes off and put them in a pile near where the scuba gear was kept, huddling next to the pool as Uncle Drake showed them each part of the scuba gear. He reminded them that scuba stood for self-contained underwater breathing apparatus and to take the lesson very seriously. Most children should be at least 12 years old, but because Sophie and Scottie were 11½, he felt that they could handle scuba diving.

"This is the oxygen tank, which is held to your body by the buoyancy control device (BCD). As you can see, it is like a harness or vest that the tank is strapped to. This should never be taken off while you two dive."

Uncle Drake was very thorough with the lesson, teaching them how to use the mask, fins, snorkel, air regulator, etc., and soon they were all in the pool diving. He taught them hand signals that meant different things (because no one can talk underwater) and rules of how long to dive by looking at the oxygen gauges and dive watch, which measures diving time. Once the girls understood all of this information, they were ready for the lagoon.

"Alright girls, we're now ready for the lagoon, so I'll go first and you follow me," Uncle Drake ordered. "We'll swim to our left to make sure we stay in this safe area."

As they swam in the lagoon, each girl touched the top of her head to signal that she was okay. Sophie and Scottie were so excited because this felt like they'd been scuba diving their entire lives. Maddie was at the lower viewing area. The girls waved to her and she gave them a thumbs-up sign. They'd have to remember to kick their legs and fins to glide from one area to the next instead of using their arms as regular swimmers do.

As they were standing on the bottom of the lagoon, another diver went whizzing by them on something the girls had never seen before. It was like a scooter with handle bars, but the diver puts their knees on its base instead of standing on it. There weren't any wheels, but some kind of propulsion system that powered the scooter forward. Scottie just stared and pointed toward it. The diver must have noticed them because he turned it around as if on a bike and pointed to it and then to the girls while looking at Uncle Drake. He gave the diver the okay symbol with his hand as if to say it was fine to let the girls try it. Scottie kicked forward with her fins, signaling that she wanted to go first. The power throttle was on the handle bars and it was very easy for her to learn how to ride it. Then Sophie had her turn.

At first, it began to sink because she was being too careful. But soon she got the hang of it too, gliding almost to the surface and then down again. As Sophie came back to where the group was standing, she handed the scooter back to the diver and he was on his way with the otter not far behind him!

"Wow, that was amazing!" Scottie announced as she took her air regulator out of her mouth and swam toward the ladder to get up onto the dive room floor.

Uncle Drake was already out of the water and reaching over to help the girls out.

"Congratulations, you two did great!" he proclaimed while helping them to get their BCD off their backs.

"It felt like we were flying in the water," Sophie said in almost a dreamy voice. "I could definitely do that again."

"Me too," Scottie chimed in. "When can we dive again?"

"We'll have to ask Maddie that question. She's waiting for us in the OI86 cafeteria, so go get rinsed and dried off over in the shower area. Your clothes are in those dressing rooms next to the showers as well."

The girls had puzzled looks on their faces, but did as Uncle Drake instructed.

"We have clothes over there?" Scottie asked Sophie as they were drying themselves off.

"I guess so. Let's go see," Sophie answered.

Just as Uncle Drake had said, the girls had a whole new set of clean clothes, undergarments, khaki shorts, a blue top for Scottie and a green for Sophie, and flip-flop sandals.

"Uncle Drake thinks of everything," Scottie stated with a smile.

"I think this was more Auntie Jill reminding him to be sure and get us the right kind of clothes for this place," Sophie said.

As the girls finished dressing and brushing their hair, Uncle Drake knocked on their door to see if they were ready to go eat. As soon as he said "eat," the girls were out in a flash and ready to head for the cafeteria. Uncle Drake told one of the gear attendants where his ATV was so that their dirty clothes and swimsuits would be put in a bag and delivered to his vehicle while they met Maddie.

"That underwater scooter was a lot of fun!" Scottie exclaimed as they all walked back to the lobby of the building.

"I'll say. I've never seen anything like it, not on TV or anywhere!" Sophie agreed.

"And you probably won't either because the special lithium-ion batteries that power the scooters haven't been invented yet at home," Uncle Drake commented. "This is the only place in time and in the world that those aqua scooters exist. In fact, the engineers on this island are also working on a sky scooter to be used no higher than 100 feet in the air. I haven't seen one on a test flight yet, but I hope I will soon. Now girls, follow me."

Uncle Drake led Sophie and Scottie out of the lobby through a hallway that entered into a massive building.

"Wow, this is like an airport terminal," Scottie observed.

"You are almost correct," Uncle Drake said. "This is the shuttle station that leads to the cafeteria. We enter that shuttle pod over there, and that will take us to food!"

As soon as he said that, the girls laughed and a cylinder-shaped object instantly slid up to the platform that they were standing on. The door of the shuttle opened and they all walked in and took a seat inside. As soon as they all were securely inside, the shuttle doors closed with a swooshing sound and they were off, as if they were sliding down a slight hill.

Windows on each side of the shuttle let the girls see out as they entered what seemed like a long hallway. As they looked out to the right, Sophie and Scottie could see all sorts of people working in various rooms lining the hallway. There were no doors. Everyone moved freely from one room to the next as needed, and Sophie noticed that all of the offices had windows. At that point, they were now under the surface of the lagoon. In fact, they could now look to their left and observe coral and fish as far as the eye could see.

"This is beautiful," Sophie commented. It reminded her of the clear part of the lava tube that they were just in the day before.

Soon the pod began to slow and the doors opened. They all got out and Uncle Drake showed them the way from the platform to the cafeteria. Once again, it was as if they were in a mini version of the terminal that they had just left, with floor to ceiling windows all around them.

"Oh good, I'm glad you all could make it for dinner. We eat a little earlier here because this is a perfect spot to see what's going on in the ocean 8.6 kilometers from the shore line," Maddie said as she greeted them.

"This place is amazing!" both girls announced at once.

"Well, get your tray and plates full of food and I'll meet you at the table over there," Maddie said, pointing to a table next to a wall of glass that allowed unobstructed views of the lagoon and ocean floor beyond.

"So tell me about what's been going on down here?" Uncle Drake asked as the girls settled into their chairs to start eating.

"Well, what do you all notice about the water?" Maddie began.

"I can see everything perfectly, as if the water wasn't even there and everything was floating or swimming in air," Sophie observed. "It's so beautiful out there."

"Yes, it's like looking at an undersea rainbow with all of the colorful coral. Except over in that spot," Scottie pointed, "it looks kind of cloudy and, well, dried out."

"You two are correct," Maddie replied. "In fact, we have the clearest and cleanest salt water on Earth, and we are still studying what makes the water this clear. But something has changed in that area and we haven't found the problem yet. You see the currents and the tides are causing a lot of confusion with our sea animals and I expect the water as well."

"How so?" Uncle Drake asked.

"We seem to be getting a lot more types of fish than usual that are staying in this area instead of migrating with the ocean currents. We also have predators that are new to this area as well and are staying in our local waters way too long. In fact, there is one now."

Scottie and Sophie looked up to see a huge sea creature glide right past them as they were eating. It was the same type of fish the girls had seen in the clear

117

part of the lava tube. Its body was a dark gray color and its head looked like the head of a hammer, only this head had eyes on the ends of each side.

Maddie noticed the girls were staring wide-eyed at the creature and said, "That huge fish that you see is called a hammerhead shark and is probably 14 feet long. They usually swim in schools during the day, so this one must be scouting around for an early dinner." They nodded their heads slowly and Maddie continued, "For some reason, these sharks usually come around about now and stay well into the night, breaking away from each other as it gets darker and becoming solitary hunters. Therefore, no one is allowed to dive past this time frame."

"It's almost as if something is feeding them. I mean, I know that our sheep at the ranch come running when they know that its dinner time," Sophie said with a smile.

"Well, we're not sure what's keeping them here, but it is annoying when we're trying to take water data samples in the areas that look dried out," Maddie commented.

"I see what you mean. We'll have to be very careful when we dive tomorrow," Dr. Drake said while looking at the girls and out into the edge of the lagoon and beyond into the ocean.

Suddenly, just as he said that, a small furry animal came up to the glass where they were eating and looked right at the girls, swirled around a few times like a ballerina, and then was gone!

"It's that otter we saw earlier!" Scottie almost shouted.

"Yes, we've noticed that this animal has made our lagoon his home," Maddie said with a smile. "We've assumed that he got caught in the unusual currents we've been having and showed up about 6 months ago. We call him Otto. I know, not very creative but what do you want from a bunch of research scientists?"

The girls laughed and looked around the cafeteria a little more. Sophie noticed that one of the OI86 personnel was up on a type of platform by an area of windows away from any tables. Maddie noticed her looking at it.

"That's one of our viewing areas for daily studies of the lagoon and ocean floor. You two girls can take those stairs up to the platform if you'd like," Maddie suggested.

Sophie and Scottie glanced at Uncle Drake and he nodded as if to say it was okay.

As the girls walked up the stairs to get to the platform, they noticed a large fish swim by them rather quickly.

"What was that?" Scottie asked as she ran up the last two steps to get a better look.

"I'm not sure, but with the window being floor to ceiling all around us we're sure to see it if it comes by again," Sophie answered

The sisters found themselves searching the water for that animal, not being sure why or what they might see. Suddenly, it swam past them again and then came back, stopping right in front of them!

"It's a dolphin, and it's beautiful!" Sophie exclaimed.

The large animal was a sleek blue-gray, no, more like a purple-blue-gray with a white underbelly like dolphins have. It had a high forehead, or melon, a long beak that always looked like there was a smile coming from it, and front flippers that seemed to be waving as it steadied itself in front of them. It seemed to have eyes that twinkled at the edge of its "smile." Bubbles were coming out from the top of its head through the blowhole, and then it swam away again.

"That is our lagoon pet," Maddie told them as she walked over to where they were standing on the platform. "We've named her Bubbles because of the bubbles that are constantly coming out of her blowhole. She used to work for the military, but she was too busy playing and not paying attention, so the navy gave her to us. Bubbles usually doesn't swim by here at this time, but is usually seen from the cafeteria window wall in the morning just as it gets light here on the lagoon's edge. Bubbles likes to look inside the cafeteria. It's almost as if she's searching for something or someone."

While Maddie was looking up and talking with the girls, Bubbles swam back to where the girls stood. She seemed to be looking right at them. In fact, Scottie felt as if Bubbles was looking right at her. Soon the dolphin was letting out bubbles and then shaking her head back and forth. She did this in front of Scottie several times, almost mesmerizing her.

"It looks like she might have seen you two scuba diving and was so curious that here she is looking at you," Uncle Drake commented as he walked over to the platform as well.

Suddenly, Otto swam by Bubbles, did a quick turn around, and tapped Bubbles on one of her fins as if to say "let's go," and they both were out of sight in seconds.

"Well, I'll be, it looks like Bubbles and Otto are friends," Maddie observed as the girls walked down the stairs of the platform to where she and Uncle Drake were standing.

"You never know what the ocean will show us. We just sometimes have to sit back and marvel at all of the undersea activity," Uncle Drake commented with a smile. "Okay, girls, time to go back to the ranch to check on the horses and get some ice cream when you're done brushing them!"

"Thank you so much for showing us around Miss McKenzie, I mean Maddie," Sophie said as Maddie walked them to catch the return shuttle pod back to the front lobby.

"Can we come back here?" Scottie asked, looking at Uncle Drake and then toward Maddie.

"Of course, you can any time," Maddie answered before Uncle Drake could say anything. "This cafeteria is always open so the research personnel can eat and work when they want to. In fact, I've made a badge for each of you. Just put it around your neck and you'll have access to OI86 and the shuttle pods."

Sophie and Scottie took their badges and put them on like necklaces. The badges had their pictures on them and their contact sponsor, which was Maddie McKenzie.

"I feel so official," Sophie commented while looking at her badge.

"Me too," Scottie agreed with a smile.

"There is a shuttle bus that goes from the ranch and other parts of the island to OI86. It leaves every 15 minutes and begins daily at 5 a.m.," Maddie added.

"Wow, that's early," Sophie remarked.

"Yes, we all seem to work many hours here, but it is a labor of love. It seems to be pretty empty here early in the morning. We all realize that we need to sleep too!" Maddie chuckled.

"Thanks again for your time," Uncle Drake said as they stepped into the shuttle. The doors quickly closed and they were on their way back. "Maddie told me that she thinks the moon's gravitational pull may also be affecting these tides, as well as the wind changes that affect the currents."

"How can that be?" Sophie asked.

"The moon has an amazing gravitational pull. If you look at the ocean from outer space, it almost looks like the ocean water is bulging out toward where the full moon is in the universe," Uncle Drake explained. "It seems as if the tides are too high for too long or…"

"Too low for too long," Scottie chimed in.

"That's right. So we need to figure out what is going on and hopefully correct this 'bulge' effect, which the researchers on this island think is also changing the trade winds. In fact, the winds seem to be dying down, which also is changing the ocean currents so the fish are basically stopping here in our outer ocean and lagoon," Uncle Drake explained.

"And too many fish means not enough food for them in the island's local waters and then too many sharks come to feed on all of the fish," Sophie figured out as she was talking.

"Very smart, Sophie," Uncle Drake commented.

"And too many fish means too many fishing boats

coming to this area as well," Scottie chimed in with a knowing smile.

"I knew you two would be perfect for solving this ocean mystery," Uncle Drake said as he helped them out of the shuttle pod.

Sophie then began, "With all of these crazy ocean current problems, I'd say..."

"Something's fishy!" both girls blurted out at the same time.

"I would also say that let's think about it tomorrow after we've brushed the horses and had some ice cream, right Uncle Drake?" Scottie asked.

Uncle Drake laughed as they headed for the ATV and the ranch. Soon they were back in the stables, brushing the horses and giving them some sweet apples as a treat. Once finished, Sophie ran back to the ATV to get the bag with their swimsuits and dirty play clothes from earlier in the day and met back up with Scottie and Uncle Drake near the stables. Scottie signaled to Sophie to walk faster toward where they were waiting for her so they could get their ice cream. After they ate their cold and extra creamy treat, all headed for their yurts to get some sleep.

As the girls were in bed and Sophie was drifting off to sleep, she heard a loud voice.

"That's it!" Scottie yelled as she sat up in bed.

"What are you talking about?

"I've been really bothered about what Bubbles was doing over and over again with the bubbles and then shaking her head back and forth, and I think I figured it out." Scottie turned on the light, climbed down the upper bunk bed ladder, and continued, "Bubbles was saying something! Quick, hand me that pad of paper and pencil over there. Yes, I'm pretty sure it was ...---.... Sis, that means SOS in Morse code!"

CHAPTER TEN

Morse of Course!

"What do you mean Morse code?" Sophie asked, rubbing her eyes so she could focus on the piece of paper Scottie was scribbling on.

"Remember just before school got out and we were learning about early ways of communicating?" Scottie asked while not waiting for an answer. "Well, one of the ways was by telegraph, and telegraphs use a code of dots and dashes that represent short and long electromagnetic pulses."

"Gosh, Scottie, I'm impressed," Sophie complimented. "I thought you'd be bored with all of that tech talk!"

"Actually, I thought it was boring at first, but when we learned about Samuel Morse being one of the developers of the telegraph, I thought it was pretty cool," Scottie replied. "I never thought that we'd use it, but when Miss McKenzie talked about Bubbles once being trained in the navy, well it all made sense because the telegraph has been used to communicate in the military for many years. Maybe they were trying to train her with Morse code and didn't realize that Bubbles actually understood it!"

"You know something, sis, I think you are on to something."

"So do I. That's why we need to go back to OI86's cafeteria first thing in the morning, Sophie."

"Okay, but what do we say to Uncle Drake?

"We'll write him a note and put it under his door before we catch the first shuttle to the institute," Scottie suggested. "We'd better get some sleep because we have to get up early in the morning."

"That's fine, Scottie, but if Bubbles doesn't show up, we need to go back to the plumeria grove to see if we can get into the lava tube. We have to find Maptrixter!"

"I know, Sophie. I'm worried about the map too. We'll go back to find it if Bubbles doesn't swim by the cafeteria," Scottie promised while climbing back up the bunk bed ladder to go to sleep.

Sophie awoke to see Scottie climbing down the ladder. Quickly, the sisters got dressed and were ready to go. Scottie had written a note to Uncle Drake saying they decided to go to OI86 first thing in the morning to watch the ocean activity and would meet him for breakfast in the cafeteria.

"I'm sure Uncle Drake will be fine with us going to the institute this early. Now that we have official badges to enter the lobby and shuttle pod, everything should go smoothly," Scottie said while putting her badge around her neck and also getting her backpack with paper and pen.

"I hope you're right, sis. I don't want to get into any trouble."

Just as Maddie had described, the shuttle bus picked up the girls and another research student exactly at 5 a.m. for a ride to OI86. The student said hello and then listened to music on what looked like two mini microphones that went right into her ears. They knew it was music because she was bobbing her head up and down as if she were at a concert. Both girls giggled a little bit and sat back for the duration of the trip. As the three got off the bus, Sophie looked at Scottie as if to ask "now what?" Scottie pointed to the student and both watched what she did with her badge and then did the same by standing in front of a camera-like digital eye that scanned their badges. They heard a voice wishing them good morning and the lobby door slid open. Luckily for the girls, the shuttle pod was moving up to the platform and they got right on and sat down.

Sophie noticed a directory posted in the front of the pod: press one to stop at the Biology Department, press two to stop at Chemistry, and so on. On the arm rest was an electronic number pad for entering the number for where they wanted to be dropped off. She checked for other departments listed and read Library, Oceanography, Geology, Seismology, and other areas of science being researched here on the island. There wasn't anyone else on the pod, so they could sit anywhere they wanted to. Sophie chose to sit closest to the inner window to see where those departments were inside the long hallway building. She noticed lots of offices, coffee and snack stands, and social areas. Just past the library, the pod began to slow and stop next to the cafeteria platform. They left the pod, walked directly up the stairs to the viewing platform of the cafeteria, and waited for any signs of Bubbles.

"I wonder how long we'll have to wait," Scottie whispered as if not to attract attention to themselves up on the platform.

"I guess we wait until there are too many people in the cafeteria for breakfast. We don't want to attract attention to ourselves because I don't know how to answer yet when someone asks us if the dolphin is talking to us," Sophie answered sarcastically.

Just as she said that, a very fast something swam right past the girls.

"What was that?"

"I'm not sure, but it was big!" Sophie exclaimed as she looked out toward the shadowy lagoon water and ocean beyond.

Just as they were straining to see out in the water, the large object stopped right in front of them. It was Bubbles!

"I can't believe she's back and remembers us," Sophie stated in a disbelieving tone.

"I knew she'd come back," Scottie assuredly replied. "Okay, Bubbles, what else do you want to tell us?"

As if on cue, Bubbles began to release bubbles in a pattern and shake her head.

"Quick, write it down, write it down," Sophie ordered while almost jumping up and down. "Wait, where is she going?"

Bubbles left the girls standing there and then quickly came back.

"Whew, she's back," Scottie said with a sigh. "I think she had to go get air and then come back to give us more letters. I hope she can stay here for a while and do this. It's hard to see what kind of pattern her bubbles and head shakes are making."

Sophie looked at the paper as Scottie wrote down what she thought were dots and dashes. Soon she could see a pattern forming on the paper.

"I think you've got it!" Sophie excitedly announced.

"Good, because I think Bubbles is tired and so am I," Scottie said and then walked down the platform steps to sit at a table and look at what she'd written.

Bubbles followed them as both girls sat down. They were looking at the paper and then back at Bubbles. Sophie thought to give her a sign that all was okay and gave her the diving hand signal by making a zero shape with her pointing finger and thumb with her other three fingers pointed up. It seemed to work because Bubbles nodded her head forward and back and was then gone.

"What did you do, sis?" Scottie asked in a concerned way.

"I gave Bubbles the okay signal that we learned yesterday while diving," Sophie replied. "So now what does it say?"

"I don't know. I only know the dots and dashes for SOS," Scottie explained, rolling her eyes.

"You don't know! That doesn't do us any good!" Sophie almost yelled, which drew some attention from those eating breakfast in the cafeteria.

"Somehow, we'll have to find a book on Morse code."

"Hmm, I know. We can walk to the OI86 library. I noticed it just before the shuttle pod slowed down, so it can't be too far from here," Sophie suggested.

"We'd better hurry then. Uncle Drake will be here in a little while and I don't want to tell him about Bubbles until we're sure she's saying more than SOS to us," Scottie replied as she put on her backpack and started to walk toward the exit of the cafeteria.

Sophie was right. The girls walked about 10 yards and they were at the entrance to the massive library. They used an electronic book source and found several books on Morse code. Sophie put in the number assigned to the book and soon one came up out of what looked like a mini table next to where the girls were standing.

"Now that's service!" Scottie announced. She quickly took the book and found a table to see what kind of pattern the dolphin had made with its bubbles and head shakes.

Sophie knew this would take a while, so she walked out toward the opening of the library and noticed an old poster on the wall. She thought that was odd, and then realized it was an original poster made from a picture of Amelia Earhart. She was standing in front of a silver dual-propeller plane, smiling as she turned to look at the camera, which showed off her kind eyes and long slim nose. She had short-cropped hair parted on the side and wore long pants with a long-sleeved blouse accessorized with a scarf around her neck. Sophie thought that Amelia sure would be tickled to know that an island was named after her.

Once she got to the library entrance, Sophie stood guard to make sure Uncle Drake didn't get to the cafeteria before them. It was easy to find out who was coming to breakfast because the last stop of the shuttle pod was the cafeteria and she could see who was getting off of the pod and onto the unloading platform before walking into the food area.

"Are you done yet?" Sophie asked, walking back to Scottie and sitting next to her. "There are more people coming for breakfast, so Uncle Drake will be here at any time."

"There, I think I've got it," Scottie said, showing the paper full of dots and dashes to Sophie. "You see we've got three dots, three dashes, one dash, three dashes again, two dashes, and then one bubble, I mean one dot. So if my coding is correct, she is saying f o l o m e."

"What in the heck does folome mean," Scottie said to more to herself than to Sophie.

"Maybe we need to put a space in the letters," Sophie suggested.

"Okay, fo lome. Or maybe she forgot a letter and the words are for lome," Scottie wrote down.

"Either way, neither of those is a word that makes sense or is even a real word," Sophie observed. "I know, let's add a space here. How about folo me?"

Both girls then looked at the word, looked at each other, and shouted, "Follow me!"

"Oh, my gosh, Bubbles wants help and needs us to follow her!" Scottie almost shouted.

Sophie agreed. "What we need to do is eat breakfast as soon as possible and get out in that lagoon. I hope Uncle Drake wants to take us diving again today."

"How do we tell him about Bubbles' message for us?" Scottie wondered as she put the book back on the return shelf and grabbed her backpack.

"We don't tell him. Uncle Drake will just have to find out where to follow Bubbles when we find out as well," Sophie answered as they walked back.

Just as they got to the cafeteria, Uncle Drake stepped out of the pod.

"Perfect timing girls. Let's go eat because I'm starved!" Uncle Drake joked as they went to get their breakfast.

As they ate, all three talked about the fish and other creatures outside the cafeteria window.

"Was it worth getting up so early to come here and observe the lagoon waters?" Uncle Drake asked.

"Boy, was it ever!" Scottie exclaimed. "We'd love to go diving again if possible."

"Yes, but I don't think I can go out today. Things have come up at the ranch I need to tend to," Uncle Drake answered. Seeing the disappointment on the girls' faces, however, he said, "But I do believe that if you girls stay in the shallow waters of the lagoon, you can dive without me. Several other research divers will be out today and can keep an eye on you."

"That sounds good to us," Scottie replied for her and Sophie.

"Then let's go to the dive room and get you two situated. I want to see you both do a test dive in the pool to make sure you remember what I taught you yesterday. If you two pass, you can go out and dive into the lagoon. To make sure you are extra safe, you will also be riding an aqua scooter," Uncle Drake said as they headed for the shuttle pod.

Both girls pumped their fists and mouthed 'yes!' to each other as they followed their uncle. Soon they were all headed back toward the dive room so they could get into their diving gear.

Uncle Drake could see that each girl took diving and safety while diving very seriously. After he tested them in the pool on all aspects of diving, Uncle Drake reminded them to be sure and check their air gauges often and to never split up while in the water.

"Okay, girls, you've passed my test. Have a great dive and I will see you for an early dinner back at the ranch."

Sophie and Scottie were able to get their aqua scooters quickly upon entering the water as there were several tied up on what looked like a floating wood platform. The scooter attendant easily dropped a scooter for each girl into the water. He showed the girls how to turn them on, and soon they were on their way toward the area that Bubbles and Otto had been in yesterday.

The girls rode their scooters side by side and kept looking for Otto and Bubbles. Their masks had clear sides, so they could easily see all around. They decided to follow the OI86 building and found themselves next to the cafeteria window, which is where the lagoon and the ocean floor meet. Suddenly, there was a strange undertow of some kind and both girls were whisked out to the open waters of the ocean. They knew to stay calm or their breathing would use up the air in their tanks before they could get back to the lagoon. But it was no use; the current was too strong for the aqua scooter and they could barely see the OI86 building.

To make matters worse, the girls were in the path of a giant whale shark whose mouth was open about 4 feet wide. Its skin was a dark gray with light-yellow markings, and it looked to be at least 45 feet long! The shark had no idea the girls weren't food and continued to suck masses of water to fill its mouth. The aqua scooters seemed to be standing still as they were getting sucked into the shark's path. Sophie and Scottie were breathing really hard now and thought this was it. They were about to become shark food.

As the girls closed their eyes and were bracing themselves for the worse, nothing happened. Both looked back and saw Bubbles nudging the gentle giant to change its course and swim about two feet past the girls. Then Otto actually swam past Sophie and around Scottie, pulling Scottie's arm as if to say "follow me!"

The girls were in shock a little bit, but calmed down and looked at their air gauges to see what they had left. They were completely empty. No oxygen was left in their tanks!

Sophie spit out her regulator and began to scream underwater, trying to get to the water surface as quickly as possible. Scottie followed her but they were too far below. Neither girl could hold her breath any longer and took a long and deep breath of the ocean water. And then, nothing—nothing at all! The girls floated on their aqua scooters under the ocean surface with their eyes closed. Scottie felt another nudge and realized it was Otto looking at her and wondering what was taking them so long.

Sophie screamed again and then, stunned, looked at Scottie. Both girls stared at each other and began to smile and then to laugh. This was their talent on Amelia Island. They could both breathe underwater! In fact, it was as if they weren't underwater at all.

"Are you okay, Scottie?" Sophie asked as she steered her scooter next to hers.

"I'm fine. I've never felt better!" Scottie replied with a giggle.

Bubbles swam up to them and looked at the girls in what seemed like disbelief, and instantly she was off swimming toward the lagoon. Otto came up to Sophie, put his front paw-like hands on what looked like his hips, tapped her head, and then swam off to follow Bubbles.

"I think we can follow them on our scooters. The undercurrent isn't so strong anymore," Sophie suggested.

Quickly, the girls turned their aqua scooters around and steered toward where Bubbles and Otto were headed.

CHAPTER ELEVEN

The Coral Cavern

The cafeteria section of the OI86 building came into view and they noticed that Bubbles and Otto swam to the right of the building and around a rock formation at the edge of where the lagoon and the ocean floor meet. The kelp beds in this area were quite thick and it was hard for the girls to keep up with their ocean friends. Scottie's scooter seemed to slow down a bit and just couldn't keep up with the others. She looked around the flowing fingers of the kelp and noticed something on the ocean floor. As the sunlight filtered through the crystal clear water, there it was in a shallow crevice barely visible among the seaweed and foraging fish all around it.

"What's going on?" Sophie asked as she turned back to find Scottie.

"Look down there, Sophie. I think I've found something that's not supposed to be here," Scottie replied. "Let's get closer, but stay out of sight."

Sophie was about to say no, but Scottie was already heading toward the object.

"I don't believe it!" Scottie blurted out.

"What, what is it?"

"It's a submarine and look what it says on the top of it," Scottie said. "Zooger Sea Exploration!"

"I can't believe he's here on this island," Sophie stated in disbelief. "Professor Zooger was able to escape from the cave with all of the butterflies he had kidnapped in Mexico and now he shows up here?"

"I know," Scottie replied as she shook her head. "I'm sure he's up to no good, so we're going to have to tell Uncle Drake."

Just then, one of Professor Zooger's divers swam by the girls but didn't see them. He had what looked like some kind of large floating barrel being pulled by a long rope, as well as a very sharp-looking pick in the other hand.

"We can't stay here and watch what he's doing with that barrel. It will get too late and Otto and Bubbles will wonder what happened to us," Sophie said.

"You're right. I'm sure we will see Professor Z again," Scottie agreed and they turned their scooters to the direction they thought Bubbles went.

The girls passed several rock formations and then just as they were about to give up, they saw Otto come up from what looked like a shipwreck of a very old wooden ship. They carefully steered their scooters into the opening and found themselves in the darkness of the ship's hull. A light attached to each scooter automatically came on and allowed them to see where they were going. They followed Otto even lower into the ship and saw an opening that led to where the scooters wouldn't fit. Leaving the scooters wedged between the rotting wood of the ship and the ocean floor, they continued to follow the small animal into what looked like another opening above them. The girls swam up and found themselves popped out of the water and next to a shallow platform, almost like surfacing out of their pond and onto their dock.

"What is this place?" Scottie asked as she took off her mask.

"I don't know, but it's beautiful," Sophie replied as she took off her mask and her scuba gear.

Both girls walked off of the shallow rock platform and stood up. The space was enormous. As the girls looked around, they could see a three-foot-wide trail that wound back and forth around what seemed like mini pools of water, gradually going up a slight incline or hill. The various colors of the sandy floor seemed to sparkle.

"This place must be as big as three barns put together," Sophie observed.

"I think so, and besides the floor, look at the walls, so smooth with swirling colors of pink, red, orange, and white," Scottie also observed while touching the smooth colors and looking around. "I wonder where Otto went and I never saw Bubbles in the shipwreck either."

Just as Scottie stated this, she and Sophie noticed someone walking toward them.

"Oh my," Sophie said, catching her breath, "I've seen this woman before!"

Both girls stood very still as this young woman slowly walked up to them. She was dressed in a simple shirt and a flowing skirt and said with a smile, "I believe this is yours."

Sophie's jaw dropped as she took the object from the woman's hand and looked at it. "Maptrixter!" she shouted in excitement.

"Wow, how did you know this was ours, and how did you get it?" Scottie asked, looking at her and thinking she did look familiar.

"This is my home," the woman stated, holding out her arm as she turned around to gesture that the entire "room" was hers. "I call it the coral cavern because it is made completely of beautiful polished coral and rainbow-colored sand."

"But how did you get here and who are you?" Sophie now asked.

"Why," she said with a giggle, "I swam here just like you. I believe you have named me Bubbles."

When the girls heard this, they both jumped backward a little in disbelief.

"What do you mean 'we' named you Bubbles? Bubbles is a dolphin," Scottie stated.

"Yes, I know," she said with a smile.

"Just a minute here," Sophie interrupted. "Are you saying that in the ocean you are a dolphin, but in this, uh, coral cavern you are a human?"

"That's right," she answered. "And what's so crazy about that? You two can breathe underwater. Gosh, I can't do that!"

"Turning from Bubbles into a human is awfully hard to believe," Scottie said. She then realized where she'd seen this woman and elbowed Sophie.

"Ouch, what was that for?"

"She's the person in that poster in the library," Scottie said in a whisper.

Instantly, Sophie recognized her and stepped back again. Sophie also realized that she was the mysterious woman she had seen during the cattle round-up.

"I'm not here to harm you two," the woman said, as she could tell the girls were a little frightened. "I need your help and I would also like to know your names."

Just as she said that, Maptrixter began to twirl in Sophie's hand as if to say that everything is all right.

"My name is Scottie and her name is Sophie," Scottie said as she turned to Sophie. "Now, what kind of help do you need?"

"Please follow me and let me show you around this cavern. As you can see there are tide pools all over the floor of this cavern, and I am the keeper of them. But I have found that something is happening to the pools. It's as if they are drying out because the tide and currents have been disrupted in some way."

"Why are these pools so important?" Sophie asked.

"Oh, you silly otter, this is no time for gifts," the woman said as Otto came up to the girls and gave each of them a beautiful gold necklace with jewels of many colors.

She then picked up Otto like a puppy, gave him a hug, and said, "The pools are important because they filter the water that makes our lagoon and ocean so pure and clear. This amazing water allows all of the sea creatures to grow and multiply. In fact, without this clear water, I believe the island will eventually die out along with the ocean waters beyond."

"That would be horrible!" Scottie exclaimed. "But what do you mean by 'they' when you talk about the pools?"

"The pools have special coral of all colors growing in them. As the single-cell algae live in the coral, the sunlight then filters from above and washes the coral with much needed sunlight, which causes the algae to produce food for the coral."

"I think that is a form of photosynthesis," Sophie commented.

"Yes, and this also allows the coral to perform some type of filtering in these pools that I don't quite understand. It's as if the coral is releasing special fresh water that you or I can drink for a short period of time and then it gets mixed in with the salt water of the lagoon and ocean waters."

"You can drink the water out of these pools?" Scottie asked as she looked into one of the tide pools.

"Yes, the purification process happens instantly and the water stays fresh until just after the sparks happen. Would you like to try some?"

"Sure," both girls answered at the same time but not really understanding what she meant by sparks flying.

"This water is really good! Hey, look at those silver-looking lines in the rock of the pools," Scottie commented. "Those lines look like the silver ones I saw in the dried river bed of the Sleeping Giant Mountain."

"I'm not sure what the lines are made of, but the color never changes and is just beautiful, don't you think?"

Sophie and Scottie nodded their heads in agreement as they sipped more fresh water.

"So," Scottie began, "the result of the filtered ocean water in these pools causes the surrounding island water to remain super clear."

"That is correct," Bubbles agreed.

"How do you know as much as you do about the coral, and how do you know how to speak our language?" Sophie asked with a puzzled look on her face.

"Well, come with me and I will show you," Bubbles said as she began to walk on the cavern trail.

"Wait, I don't know if we can help you, but we need to call you something other than Bubbles!" Sophie stated. "You look just like a person in a large picture that we saw earlier today. Can we call you Amelia?"

"You mean for the island?"

"Yes, I guess you could say that," Sophie answered while looking at Scottie.

"Good then, Amelia it is! Now come with me and I'll show you how I learned to speak English. You can also tell me what you know about the island. It is very hard for me to leave the cavern to go on the island because sometimes people see me and look a little shocked and I don't know why."

"What do you mean by leaving the cavern?" Scottie asked.

"What was that?" Sophie interrupted.

Both girls could hear a loud boiling and splashing sound from the farthest pool, which was at the highest point of the cavern floor. They realized it was seawater, and it came gushing into the top pool, and began to overflow like a waterfall into the next lower one, and so on, until the water reached the lowest pool that the girls were standing nearest. The water sounded soothing but loud. After the commotion, the real action began!

"Oh, my gosh, it's as if we're at a New Year's Eve celebration with fireworks set off above all of the pools!" Scottie announced.

The girls could hardly believe what they were seeing. Mini fireworks were everywhere, some bursting over their heads. Then a thin film of jeweled sand settled on their hair and arms. The cavern floor was also covered with a thin layer of what looked like multicolored glittery sand.

"What just happened?" Sophie asked in a shocked voice.

"Those, Sophie and Scottie, were the pools being filled up from the high tide, which starts the filtration process," Amelia described. "It usually happens every day, but now only happens every other day, which is starting to worry me."

"But what were the fireworks about?" Scottie asked.

"Oh, that is a really special effect that happens when the pools fill up and the water starts to churn up in them," Amelia began to explain. "At first, I couldn't figure out what was causing the sparks. So in the largest pool I carefully got into the water and as I became a dolphin, I noticed hundreds of tiny seahorses in the water. I also noticed that there are deep areas of the pools leading out toward the ocean. You see, below this coral cavern are crevices and alcoves that are filled with electrified moray eels. I've been researching them and they seem to have evolved and now contain thousands of electric organs that store power. When we get the rush of ocean water into the pools, the eels emit about 600 volts of electricity. I think this electricity has affected the seahorses and they have become electrified as well. Every time the water rushes in, it causes them to release their tails from the sea grasses in the pools. They brush up against the colorful corals and the interaction releases a spark that becomes the color of the coral as it travels through the water and gets released into the air. As far as I can tell, the spark causes the air to stay super pure as well, which keeps me, well, young."

"How long have you been here?" Sophie questioned.

"I'm not sure, but I think not long after the island formed."

Both girls looked at her in astonishment. That would mean hundreds of years, because it takes many, many years for a coral reef to form and a volcanic island to grow lush with plants.

"Wow, this is SO amazing. I can't believe we are seeing all of this, especially the fireworks, or as you say, the sparks," Scottie replied.

"But what makes all of this colorful sand on the floor?" Sophie asked while looking down all around her.

"That is the cooled-off spark dust, which glows in the dark and allows me to see in the cavern when the sun goes down," Amelia answered. "Now, enough of these questions and please follow me."

"You were about to tell us another way to leave the cavern," Sophie reminded Amelia.

"Oh, yes, there is another way to get to the island from this place instead of through the ocean waters. In fact, you two were on your way when you walked into the lava tube from the plumeria trees, but there was an earthquake and that is when…"

"That is when Sophie dropped the map as we ran back to the entrance to get out of there as soon as possible!" Scottie interrupted.

"That's right, so I decided to walk through the cavern, to the clear tube and finally the lava tube to see if there was any damage, and I noticed something on the ground. I took it back to the cavern and unrolled the large paper and realized it was a map of the island. You two were very clever on figuring out how to get into the lava tube."

"Well, that was an accident," Scottie explained. "I leaned on the rock and it began to move until the entrance was revealed."

"Well, I don't think anything happens by chance. You two were meant to find out about the coral caverns in one way or the other," Amelia replied.

"I'm just glad to get Maptrixter back," Sophie exclaimed with a smile while walking alongside Amelia on the trail.

"Oh, here we are. This is how I learned how to speak your language."

On the walls of this much smaller room or chamber, the girls could see nothing but books, shelves and shelves of them. Otto was following them and pulled one off the shelf. It was an English language book.

"Otto knows which ones I am always referring to. He's very smart you know," Amelia commented.

"Where did you get all of these books?" Sophie gasped.

"When I go about the island late at night I always go to the recycle bin and see what was left there. It's amazing how many old books aren't needed on this island! Earlier you mentioned the map, Sophie. I think you should unroll it because I noticed an area on the island that seems to be glowing," Amelia suggested.

Immediately, Sophie took the map and unrolled it on an old table. Sure enough, Maptrixter revealed where they were under the ocean surface and also showed a trail on the island that was glowing.

"Oh, wow!" Scottie blurted out. "I know exactly where that is. It's where Starburst got spooked and ran up the trail that took us to that strange magnetized hut."

"You mean on Earthquake Trail?" Sophie asked hesitantly.

"I wonder if there is a link between the tides and that hut in some way," Sophie said more to herself than to the others.

"I'll bet that Professor Zooger has something to do with that hut too," Scottie stated.

"That name sounds familiar. I know I've seen that name on that submarine not far from here," Amelia added. "In fact, as a dolphin I've been watching the divers that go out from there in what looks like a launching chamber and I'm really mad at them!"

"Why, what have they done?" Scottie asked.

"I believe they don't want other divers around, so they feed the sharks every day to keep them here in the outer lagoon area," Amelia observed. "But what happens is that the extra food is attracting more fish to these waters, which in turns brings too many fish and the sunlight gets blocked from reaching the coral to keep it healthy."

"Do you mean to say that Professor Z is feeding the hammerhead sharks?" Sophie asked in disbelief.

"Yes, but I'm not sure what he's up to with the sharp picks that the divers always have in their hands," Amelia added.

"I think I do," Scottie said. "I bet he's looking for more of this." And then Scottie lifted up the gold and jeweled necklace that Otto had given her.

"Is there more of this, uh, treasure around here in the cavern?" Scottie asked Amelia.

"Oh, yes!" Amelia replied in an excited voice. "Otto loves shiny objects and is constantly bringing me beautiful things. Come with me and I'll show you."

Sophie rolled up Maptrixter and both girls followed Amelia farther into the cavern, turning left into another large coral room. The girls gasped at what they saw!

CHAPTER TWELVE

Disband Z Diabolical Plan

The room had a brilliant sparkle to it and the sisters could see why. Everywhere they looked were piles and piles of treasure. There were piles of silver dishes and jeweled forks and knives. There were mirrors with frames of gold all around them. There were also piles of necklaces, bracelets, rings, and other jewelry. But what Sophie and Scottie noticed most was what was on the top of the pile— an enormous pink pearl!

"I've never seen anything like this," Sophie whispered.

Just then Scottie walked over to another treasure pile and found a beautiful diamond and pearl tiara. "Is it okay if I try this on?" she asked Amelia.

"Of course, all of this has come from the ocean. Otto has collected it all and brings it to me. I then throw it onto the pile of 'treasure' as you call it. Does this mean that this stuff is valuable?"

Both girls began to giggle and blurted out with wide eyes, "Yes!"

"Then there must be some way we can use it to get that man, uh, Professor Zooger to leave this area," Amelia said thoughtfully.

"We could somehow make a trap for him, but I think we'd better ask Uncle Drake for help," Scottie suggested.

"Who is Uncle Drake?" Amelia asked in a puzzled voice.

"Uncle Drake is a very smart man and we have helped him solve another mystery in another land. He is our uncle, is trustworthy, and will be very helpful to you, Amelia, and to this island," Sophie explained.

"He is the person who put Maptrixter in Sophie's care," Scottie added.

"Well, by all means, let's get your uncle to help. In fact, you should get back to OI86 before somebody thinks you two are missing," Amelia suggested. "I will follow you girls back to make sure you are safe. If you can, meet me before sunset at the plumeria trees with your Uncle Drake."

Sophie and Scottie nodded and began to put on their wetsuits and scuba gear. Sophie carefully put Maptrixter inside her wetsuit to make sure it didn't get wet, and Scottie put the necklaces carefully over her head before she finished putting on her wetsuit. Even though they didn't need the oxygen tanks any-more, they certainly didn't want to alarm any other divers that might notice them on their return to the dive room.

Amelia went into the water first. She sat on the platform of the coral cavern and turned over onto her stomach. Right before Sophie and Scottie's eyes she began to change into a bottlenose dolphin. First her feet turned into the flukes, and then her legs became like a dolphin's body with the dorsal fin on her back. Amelia's arms became flippers and her face became the eyes with ears on each side of her forehead, or melon. Her blowhole was right above the melon and her beak (which looked like a long nose) consisted of very sharp teeth for hunting and eating. The girls hadn't really noticed before, but Bubbles' skin had almost an iridescent purple glow to it that was quite beautiful. Both of them had to blink their eyes a couple of times to believe what they were seeing, but got into the water to follow Bubbles back to the institute.

As the girls swam into the shipwreck, Sophie noticed Otto in the water near them and he was wearing a different necklace than the ones he'd given the girls! Scottie saw Otto with his fancy new jewelry and let out a giggle. She and Sophie found their aqua scooters where they left them and were off, out of the shipwreck and heading back to the institute. Sophie noticed a shadow over her and she gasped, waving to Scottie to look up.

There they were, three hammerhead sharks swimming overhead. One spotted the girls and began to swim right for them!

"We need to go faster!" Scottie yelled to Sophie as Otto seemed to encourage them to move at top speed.

Both girls pressed the full-speed button on their scooters. The hammerhead shark was just behind the girls. As they both looked back, they noticed a large object come up at full speed and ram the shark on its soft underbelly.

"Hurry, let's get out of here!" the girls shouted to each other and continued to go as fast as they could on their aqua scooters until they were out of the shark's path.

At first, Sophie and Scottie didn't recognize what was ramming the shark, but soon realized it was Bubbles, who had turned a very dark purplish blue, almost black, as she swam around at full speed again to ram the shark with her beak. While the girls continued as fast as they could, they didn't notice Professor Zooger and another diver below them in a kelp forest watching the whole shark encounter. One of his divers pointed up at Bubbles and then at Otto, making hand gestures for Professor Z to look at what was around the otter's neck.

When the girls could see the OI86 structure, they noticed another diver coming up to them on an aqua scooter. It was Uncle Drake and he looked very concerned. He put up his hand to signal if they were okay, and they returned the hand signal and nodded yes. Scottie looked around to see if there was anyone else with him and noticed that the other divers were a little ways away. Of course, Scottie can never keep a secret when something so amazing as breathing underwater becomes a special talent and took her air regulator out of her mouth. Uncle Drake's eyes looked like they were going to pop out of his head, and he reached to put it back into her mouth!

"It's okay, Uncle Drake," Sophie said to him as he reached for Scottie. "We can breathe and talk underwater!"

Uncle Drake instantly turned toward Sophie and almost forgot to breathe himself while looking at her and then back to Scottie. He signaled for them to follow him as they headed back to the scooter platform and dive room. As he did this, Bubbles swam around them with her skin back to her normal glowing purple and blue color. She looked right at the girls and nodded her head as if to say all is well and I'll see you soon. Both girls put their hands out to pet her and in a blink of an eye, she was gone.

Uncle Drake noticed this, of course, and couldn't wait to get back to the dive room to ask the girls many questions.

Once in the dive room, Uncle Drake said, "Alright girls, after you are dried off and in your clothes we need to talk about your day. I can tell that much has happened to you two since breakfast this morning."

Both girls began to talk at once, but Uncle Drake lifted up his hand as if to say stop talking and get dressed.

While the girls changed, Maddie came down to the dive room with large bowls of frozen yogurt topped with fresh tropical fruit and nuts.

"Oh, thank you. Sophie and Scottie are going to love you for this because I'm sure they are starved," Uncle Drake said with a smile as he took the bowls from her.

"Well, I noticed that the girls must be tired. They were out there for a long time. In fact, they must be dangerously low in their oxygen tanks," Maddie commented in a concerned voice.

"Luckily for them, little girls have small lungs," Uncle Drake replied and took a bite of his yogurt. "Ah, there are our young divers now."

"Hi, Miss McKenzie. Oh, thank you. I'm starved!" Scottie exclaimed as she took a bowl of frozen yumminess for her and one for Sophie.

"Oh yum, this is perfect!" Sophie agreed.

"Did you two enjoy observing the sea life early this morning?" Maddie asked.

"Yes, we did," Sophie answered before Scottie could say anything. "It is so beautiful and calm out there."

"Well, good, I'm glad you two enjoyed it and I assume you also had fun on your second dive."

"We sure did," Scottie blurted out with a mouthful of fruit and then burped!

"Now Scottie, mind your manners," Sophie scolded.

This made Maddie and Uncle Drake laugh.

"Well, I need to go to a meeting, so enjoy your day and the snack," Maddie said with a wink and left the dive room.

"She sure is nice," Sophie commented.

"Yes, Maddie is, and I had to make sure that she didn't check your tank levels or I think SHE would've needed oxygen!"

"Oh, that's right. I don't think it would've been easy to explain our underwater, uh, talent to her," Scottie agreed.

"Yes. Now tell me everything that has happened to you two this morning."

"Everything?" both asked at the same time.

"Yes, everything," Uncle Drake stated as he noticed Sophie walking to the dressing room and coming back with Maptrixter in her hand. "You can start, Sophie, as I see you have your map back."

Sophie and Scottie told Uncle Drake about the Morse code message from Bubbles and finding the answer in the library with a large poster of Amelia Earhart hung up on one of the walls. They continued to tell him of their whale shark encounter, how scared they were, and how Bubbles helped to get the shark to swim around them.

"That is when we realized that we were breathing way too much oxygen," Scottie announced. "Yes, we were too far from the surface, so I screamed and took a breath and just kept breathing!" Sophie added in amazement.

Uncle Drake shook his head and encouraged them to continue their story.

"You mean to tell me that Bubbles and the otter wanted you to follow them and that is when you noticed a submarine that had Zooger Sea Exploration on it?" Uncle Drake asked more to himself than to the girls. "I mean, I had heard a man with a patch over one eye had been seen on the island, but couldn't believe that he'd show up again."

"Oh, it's him all right. In fact, we saw one of his thugs diving with a barrel he was pulling and a really sharp pick in his hand," Scottie described.

The girls continued to describe how they found Maptrixter and Amelia in the coral cavern. Uncle Drake couldn't believe how the cavern and its special pools were connected to the clear and perfect lagoon and ocean waters. But he really had a hard time picturing Bubbles turning into a human, realizing that anything is possible within the magic frame.

"We've been researching this water phenomenon for years, and leave it to you girls to figure it out," Uncle Drake said with a chuckle.

"Yes, but the tide pools are in danger, so that makes Amelia, the island, and the surrounding ocean waters also in danger," Sophie explained. "We're sure that Professor Z has something to do with this."

"And we also are sure that Zooger the booger has something to do with the hut too," Scottie added.

"What hut?" Uncle Drake asked.

"Instead of explaining the hut to you, we need to show you," Sophie suggested. "We would like to take a horse ride when we get back. That will be the easiest way to get there, and I'm sure the horseshoes are fixed on Starburst and Firefly by now."

"But before we get to the hut, we need to go here," Scottie pointed to Maptrixter and Sophie unrolled it.

All three could see a glowing spot on the map and then it began to blink.

"Wow, I've never seen a blinking light on Trixter before," Sophie stated. "And look, Scottie, it's blinking at the plumeria trees."

"We'd better hurry up. Come on, Uncle Drake, we've got to go!" Scottie announced in an excited tone as Sophie rolled up Maptrixter and put it into Scottie's pack.

Uncle Drake realized that the girls had discovered more things on this island than even he knew about and was soon following them out of the OI86 building and to his ATV. In no time they were back at the ranch to change into riding clothes and to saddle up the horses for their late afternoon ride.

"I think we'd better wear our bathing suits under our riding clothes, Sophie, just in case we need to dive again. Oh, and I almost forgot. I'll put these necklaces in my drawer for now. The stones seem to glow, don't you think?"

"That's a good idea, Scottie. They do seem to glow." Sophie pulled the map out of Scottie's backpack and continued, "I'll put Maptrixter in my drawer as well so it will stay warm and dry in our yurt. Do you understand, Trixter? You are NOT to follow us in any way, okay?"

The map seemed to become a little wilted as Sophie ordered it to stay in the yurt, but it didn't seem to argue, knowing that it could get too stiff and not fit into the drawer if it wanted to.

When Uncle Drake met the girls in front of their yurt, they continued to walk toward the stables. Just as they were about to pass the supplies store, two men walked out and continued in front of them by about 10 feet. Scottie noticed the men first and couldn't believe her eyes. There right in front of them was Professor Zooger and one of his thugs!

Scottie quickly pulled Sophie and Uncle Drake into the store so Professor Z wouldn't notice them.

"What are you doing, Scottie?" Sophie asked with an irritated voice.

"Look out the doorway very carefully. It's Professor Zooger!" Scottie exclaimed.

"Oh, my gosh, I didn't even notice," Sophie replied.

"Come on, Uncle Drake, we need to see where they are headed."

All three quickly walked out of the store and saw the men drive away from the parking area. They noticed the professor's ATV didn't turn on the road that led to the pier, but kept going straight past the stables and toward the dirt roads of Sleeping Giant Mountain.

Suddenly, both girls yelled out "the hut!" and began to run for the stables. All were able to saddle up their horses in record time and were riding on the dirt road that Professor Z had taken.

"We'll have to meet Amelia at the plumeria grove after we follow Professor Zooger. I hope Amelia will understand if we're a little late," Sophie shouted while galloping past the trail that led to the trees.

"Whoa, whoa," Uncle Drake shouted as he slowed his horse to a walk. "Okay, girls, the only way Professor Zooger can drive up this mountain is by using the dirt road. I have a plan. We will take the Earthquake Trail that you two were on during the cattle round-up. We know it's faster, but your horses' shoes will probably get loose again."

"That's okay, Uncle Drake. We know the way and our only option is to get there first and hide the horses before Professor Booger Head gets there," Scottie replied as they all started to gallop the horses toward the trail.

The horses were racing up the mountain so fast that the riders had to pull back quickly on the reins, making the horses stop at the end of the trail by digging in their back legs and hooves into the soft island dirt. This caused the soil to spray out similar to when a baseball player slides into base feet first. After they tied up their horses at the end of the trail, all three could hear some talking as two men walked up another trail toward the hut. Hiding among the thick vines near the hut as fast as they could, they made sure all were within earshot to hear what was being said.

"I'm telling you, boss, the magnetic hut is working just as you said it would. In fact, when do we start on phase two of your perfectly diabolical plan?" the guard asked.

"Not so fast, Lurch," the man with the eye patch and long gray hair in a ponytail began. "We need to check the magnetic beam emitting from the top of the hut. It is interacting perfectly with the moon's gravitational pull and causing a bulge just slight enough to make the tides erratic, as well as messing with the wind currents, which (begins to laugh) causes the ocean currents to deposit hundreds of species of fish into the island's ocean waters. I especially love all of the hammerhead sharks that have now made the lagoon their home," the man explained with a smile.

"Yeah, Professor Zooger, you're a real genius," Lurch responded. "But I'm telling you, we've been using the picks at the cliffs and under the water and as soon as the lab results come in, I bet they'll show that we found something."

"Yes, you may be correct on this one," Professor Z talked as if thinking out loud. "If my calculations are correct, we may have just found one of the last great veins in the Earth's crust of the most precious metals on Earth—platinum!"

"So what comes next, boss?" the thug asked.

"As the tides and currents continue to get worse and worse, this island will become too difficult to use as a research site and those who live here will have to leave. Boohoo to all of those simple researchers," the professor remarked and then laughed again.

"Sounds good, boss, but what do we do with that pesky otter we just captured?"

Both girls couldn't believe what they heard and gasped loudly. Uncle Drake quickly put his hands over each of their mouths so they would stay as quiet as possible.

"What was that?" Professor Z blurted out, looking around where they were standing.

"I didn't hear anything, boss. It was probably a bird or another critter. It gets really weird around here, and I'm thinking it's because of the constant magnetic pull of the hut."

"Hmm, maybe you're right. Lock up the control box of the hut and let's get back to the sub," he ordered in a gruff tone. "So far nobody has been able to prove I am the cause of the great tidal changes to the island and I want to keep it that way. Also, by following that otter, we've been able to discover some treasure here and there, but we always seem to lose him with that darn dolphin. But patience, my dear Lurch, has now paid off. Our good fortune in noticing the lovely silvery white metal that the otter swims by daily near the cliffs should lead to riches beyond our belief. We will also control all of the new technology that this platinum will be used in."

As soon as Lurch was done locking up the hut, both men walked back to their ATV. It was all that Uncle Drake could do to keep the girls from running out and trying to get at the two men in some way.

"We've got to get to the plumeria trees as soon as possible. I'm sure Amelia is worried sick and needs our help more than ever," Scottie said.

"Now, hold on. I want to see this hut that the professor was talking about. You see, I know how magnets work," Uncle Drake said as he walked over to the locked control box.

"What can we do?" Scottie asked, noticing the pull of her belt buckle toward the hut.

"What we need to do is disrupt the spinning electrons that orbit the thousands of millions of atoms in the magnetized iron of this hut. All of these electrons are spinning in the same direction and..."

"And if we get them to spin in different directions, then the magnetic beam that is projecting into the atmosphere will be broken," Sophie stated in a knowing tone of voice.

"That's correct. We'll need something that will basically cover the beam and then we can get to the control box and destroy it," Uncle Drake added.

"I think I know what will work, and it's large, round, and pink!" Scottie exclaimed as she ran to her horse with the others following her.

CHAPTER THIRTEEN

Eelectrifying!

S cottie, Sophie, and Uncle Drake rode their horses as fast as they possibly could down Earthquake Trail to meet with Amelia. Sophie went in front so she could lead Uncle Drake and Scottie to the plumeria trees. As the horses walked, Papaya came swooping down onto Uncle Drake's shoulder.

"Why, hello, Papaya, glad you could join us," he said with a smile.

"Uncle Drake?"

"Yes, Scottie?"

"What is platinum and why is Professor Z so excited about it?"

"Platinum is the rarest metal on Earth. It is found in what is called alluvial sand or soil from various kinds of rivers that have dried up long ago. There are probably many dried-up river beds on this island, so I wouldn't be surprised at the different types of metals that may be here. This type of metal usually isn't found near a marine setting, but I guess there isn't anything usual about this island," Uncle Drake almost muttered to himself. "Platinum," he continued, "is also nonreactive, which means it resists corrosion. In fact, pure platinum is harder than pure iron. It is an amazing substance because platinum can be compressed like a thin sheet or stretched into a wire. Some of its uses are in electrical contacts and electrodes and in dental, medical, and lab equipment. It can be used in every industry on Earth."

"I remember Ma got a ring from Pa made with platinum for one of their anniversaries. She was really happy and gave him a big hug and kiss," Scottie remembered with a bit of a sour look on her face.

"It was sweet," Sophie said with a smile.

"Oh, I'm sure Kathryn loves the ring. Very fine jewelry is made with platinum," Uncle Drake commented.

"I can see why Professor Zooger is excited about this potential discovery, but wouldn't the mining of this metal destroy the island?" Sophie asked.

"Yes, it would. Governments would possibly fight over the platinum, as Zooger would somehow control how it is mined on the island and what the price would be to the nations willing to pay the most for it," Uncle Drake explained.

"Oh, no. Amelia showed Sophie and me parts of the tide pools that look like they have silver in them. I bet that metal is platinum. We have to stop the Zooger Booger!" Scottie shouted.

"That, Scottie, is exactly what we will do!" Uncle Drake announced.

The riders stopped suddenly and saw a woman standing next to a tree.

"Amelia!" both girls announced.

"I'm so glad you have all come," Amelia exclaimed. "I desperately need your help!"

"We know about Otto, so let's hurry," Sophie said, noticing Amelia looking at Uncle Drake.

They all got off of their horses and Uncle Drake walked up to Amelia, almost staring at first and then quickly introducing himself to her.

"You must be the secretive Amelia," he began. "I am Dr. Drake and I can see why the islanders claim to have seen a ghost."

"Sophie and Scottie have said that I resemble this Amelia Earhart person that the island is named after. I feel honored."

"She was a great aviation pioneer, but my nieces have described you as a different kind of pioneer, a pioneer of the ocean," Dr. Drake said with a smile.

"Amelia, can you bring us to your cavern from here? We don't have any time to waste," Scottie said.

"Yes, please follow me."

Scottie made sure that the horses were safely tied to the plumeria trees, and Sophie noticed Papaya was safely perched on one of the tree branches. All watched Amelia as she easily reached out to touch the huge volcanic rock that moved to reveal the lava tube trail. Slowly, the boulder slid to the left with a deep grinding sound.

"Quickly, this way," Amelia urged the others.

It was still daylight, so they could see where to walk on the trail. As the lava tube walls changed from rock to clear glass, Sophie, Scottie, and Dr. Drake couldn't help but stop and look around them. The ocean currents were calm, and they could see all of the multi-colored fish, corals, and kelp beds all around them. Sophie pointed to a group of sea turtles foraging for food, easily navigating the ocean floor. Soon, they entered the coral cavern with its swirling pink, red, orange, and white walls. Uncle Drake was fascinated by what he was seeing and realized this place must never be discovered.

"This is my home, Dr. Drake. I call it the coral cavern. I am the one who makes sure that the tide pools are working correctly to ensure the island waters stay fresh and clear for all of the sea creatures who live in it."

"Scottie and Sophie told me about this place, and it truly is special. I will make sure that you won't have to defend it from the likes of Professor Zooger."

"Speaking of Professor Z, we'd better get going Amelia," Sophie suggested.

"Yes, but first we need to get Uncle Drake something," Scottie added. She then ran to the treasure room and returned with the basketball-sized pink pearl in her hands. "Will this disrupt the spinning electrons of that magnetic beam?"

"That must be the largest pearl I've ever seen," Uncle Drake stated with wide eyes while taking it from Scottie. "Yes, I think this will work perfectly.

Let's get back to the horses with the pearl and head for the ranch. I will ask Kimo for help with shutting down the hut once we put the horses in the stables."

"That sounds great, Uncle Drake, but we can't come with you," Scottie replied. "We have our suits on under our clothes and if we go with you, that will take too long and who knows what will happen to Otto."

"But your scuba gear and…"

"It's all right, Dr. Drake," Amelia interrupted. "I will make sure the girls are safe in the ocean. It is a little alarming but they really can breathe perfectly in the water."

Dr. Drake looked at the girls. "If your Auntie Jill knew what I was about to let you two girls do, she wouldn't talk to me for a week!"

"Oh, thank you, Uncle Drake. Everything will be fine," Sophie said as both girls walked up to hug him. "Scottie and I know that this is a special talent here on the island and we would never try breathing underwater at the ranch or anywhere else."

"Girls, get ready to swim and I will take your uncle back to the entrance of the lava tube. We must hurry before Otto is lost to us forever," Amelia said and began to run toward the entrance with Dr. Drake.

When Amelia got back, she showed them an old pair of fins. Each girl could use one fin and adjust it at the heel to keep it on her foot.

"Well, that will have to do and you two can also hang onto my dorsal fin if needed. I'm sure that I can swim faster than any of those aqua scooters the divers use," she said with a little chuckle.

First, Amelia laid on the rock platform that was submersed in the water and quickly turned into a dolphin. She swam around as the girls got into the water. They were a little hesitant, not being sure each could still breathe underwater. Sophie looked at Scottie and they held hands, looking at each other as they slowly put their entire bodies into the water. They took a deep breath and sure enough, they could breathe as if they were on land. A feeling of relief swept over them, but what about their eyes! As they looked around the old shipwreck, it didn't seem to matter that a mask wasn't protecting their eyes. Scottie spotted Bubbles and both girls followed the dolphin as they swam toward the Zooger Sea Exploration submarine.

Dr. Drake decided to let Starburst and Firefly go as he galloped toward the stables. The horses could sense that something was wrong and followed him and Papaya back to the ranch. The wind was starting to pick up, so it took a little more effort for Papaya to fly next to Dr. Drake and the horses. He waved to Kimo while the stable help took the horses from Dr. Drake, signaling Kimo to come over as the doctor walked to one of the ranch ATVs.

"I don't have time to explain, but our security on the island has been threatened and we have to act fast," Dr. Drake told him as they walked over to the ATV and got in. "And oh, you can hold this for me."

Kimo's eyes almost popped out of his head as he took the enormous pink pearl from Dr. Drake's hand. "What the heck! I've never seen such a large pearl. Where are we going with this?"

"We're heading for a magnetic hut in the upper grasslands of Sleeping Giant Mountain," Dr. Drake answered, and he stepped on the gas pedal to get the ATV to go as fast as possible on the rutted dirt road.

The tides were supposed to be dangerously high that night, and Dr. Drake wasn't sure how that would affect OI86 or the coral cavern. He also noticed that the winds were becoming very strong, possibly too strong for the island, and began to get a sinking feeling in his stomach. As the ATV headed up the dirt road of the mountain, the tires began to spin in the dirt as if to refuse to go any farther.

"Come on ol' girl, you've got to keep going," Dr. Drake stated as if to encourage the vehicle to keep moving.

"I can't believe how powerful the winds are. It's as if the Sleeping Giant is angry," Kimo shouted as they continued up the road, holding on to the sides of the roll bar.

Dr. Drake also worried about Sophie and Scottie and hoped that Bubbles would protect them as they tried to save Otto.

While Bubbles and the girls continued to swim away from the shipwreck, they noticed that the water currents were unusually strong. Sophie and Scottie had to hold on to the dolphin's dorsal fin to cut through the water. As they got closer to the submarine, Bubbles realized they would need help because the hammerhead sharks were now beginning to swim over them. She sat the girls down in a protected area of rock and nodded up and down to signal for the girls to stay until she got back.

"I wonder what Bubbles is up to?" Scottie asked Sophie.

"I'm not sure, but we can't really go anywhere," Sophie replied. "Hey, look up there. It looks like the hammerheads are having trouble swimming, as if their sense of direction is all messed up in this crazy current we are having."

The sharks seemed to be confused and began to bash into each other while trying to swim where Zooger's divers usually fed them. Soon they started to fight among themselves, and then as if giving up, each shark began to swim away from the area.

"Whew, those hammerheads sure are creepy. Look, Sophie. It's Zooger's men and they have Otto on some kind of a leash!" Scottie said, pointing toward the sub. "I bet they were hoping Otto would show them more of the shiny platinum veins in the cliffs."

"It doesn't look like Otto showed them anything. Look how he is struggling to get free," Sophie observed. "Let's stay on the ocean floor and follow them. I want to see where they bring Otto because he will need air soon."

"What about Bubbles? She'll get worried that we're not here," Scottie asked with a surprised tone. (Usually she is the one suggesting they leave a place that they were told to stay!)

"She'll find us. Now let's go!" Sophie ordered.

Soon the thugs could be seen swimming under some kind of room or air chamber with access to a hatch from underneath the chamber. It was attached to the side of the sub where all of them could breathe, keeping Otto alive as well. Now, the girls thought, how do we free Otto from this chamber? They also wondered if Uncle Drake was at the hut.

The wind whipped around the island with a stronger force than those on the island had ever seen. The roofs on the stables and the cafeteria were threatening to rip off at any moment. Dr. Drake knew that this wind storm must have something to do with the magnetic beam and he needed to go faster up the mountain road.

"We're almost there," he yelled to Kimo as the ATV engine was about to overheat. "There, see that overgrown trail?"

Kimo nodded as Dr. Drake pointed to the trail.

"We need to follow that trail to a hut that is overgrown with vines," Dr. Drake ordered in a loud voice over the howling wind as he pulled some large cutters from the vehicle. "Once we get there, I'll need you to hand me the giant pearl after I climb up on top of the hut. You can use these cutters to cut the lock off the control box."

"What do I do once the lock is off?" Kimo asked as they walked up the trail.

"I'll let you know as soon as I think of something! I sure hope Sophie and Scottie are okay."

As Sophie and Scottie were trying to see into the scratched glass of the air chamber, they could feel a kind of mini zap of electricity on their arms.

"What was that?" Scottie asked Sophie while rubbing her arm.

Just then, both girls looked up to the left of the submarine and noticed the sunlight in the water became eerily dim. The girls gasped, hardly believing what they were seeing.

Bubbles was leading the way and following her must have been hundreds and hundreds of eels. Some were gray, some were dark brown with white dots all over them, and some were a strange glowing green. As they got closer, half went one way and the other half went the other. Soon they were on each side of the submarine. Bubbles then swam down the middle of the eels, directly over Professor Zooger's sub. It was as if Bubbles was yelling "CHARGE!"

"I can't believe what I'm seeing," Sophie said more to herself than to Scottie.

All at once, the eels opened their mouths wide and a kind of electrical current blasted the sub. The sub started to lose all power, blowing one fuse after another and seeming to change color to a very deep and dull gray. The girls could see the divers pouring out of the sub like black ants pouring out of an ant hole! Professor Zooger's men were crammed into the air chamber with their scuba gear barely on, trying to push each other out of the way to be first to reach the bottom escape hatch of the chamber. Scottie thought they were such cowards and knew Uncle Drake would never act that way.

Meanwhile, Dr. Drake had to carefully grip the thorny vines that were clinging to the hut. As the wind gusted around him, he was almost blown off the vine, hanging on with one hand and one foot. Kimo carefully put the pearl on the ground and began to use the cutters on the metal of the padlock, his face grimacing as he tried to use both hands to cut through it.

As Dr. Drake crawled on top of the hut, he could hear a humming noise and feel a type of electrical force that made the hair on his arms stand up. As he looked to where the sound was coming from, he noticed a five-inch hole on the top of the hut and yelled, "Kimo, is the lock off yet?"

"Almost," Kimo grunted and yelled at the same time. He felt as if his muscles in his arms were going to burst. Then crash! The lock fell to the ground and he opened up the control box.

"What do you see?" Dr. Drake shouted. As he rolled onto his back, he could see dark menacing clouds swirling around in the sky. Lightning bolts darted out from one cloud to another blackened cloud, shooting this way and that way.

"There is one large black lever that is pointed up," Kimo shouted back.

"Okay, good! Now throw the pearl up to me, and on the count of three, I want you to pull the lever down."

Kimo had a pretty good throwing arm, but the wind caught the giant pearl in the air, which caused it to bounce on the roof of the hut. Dr. Drake was able to catch it just before it bounced off the roof again and out of Kimo's reach on the ground.

"Okay, are you ready?" Dr. Drake shouted again.

"Yep!"

"One…two…three!" he yelled.

Dr. Drake put the pearl over the hole, which disrupted the magnetic pull of the hut's beam. Then, seconds later, Kimo pulled the black lever down toward the ground. There was a kind of sucking sound that seemed to keep the pearl in place. The winds instantly calmed down and there was complete silence. No birds were chirping, no bugs were buzzing—nothing. Suddenly, a deep rumbling could be heard from under the Sleeping Giant and the hut began to shake beneath Uncle Drake. He knew that being on top of the hut wasn't safe and quickly started to climb down the vines. The shaking became very violent, so he decided to jump off the hut before reaching the ground. Just as he did that, a large sink hole opened up and swallowed the entire hut!

"Quick, take my hand or you'll be right behind that hut too!" Kimo yelled to Dr. Drake as he stood near the edge of the hole, holding onto another vine that was attached to some nearby trees.

As Kimo pulled him out, the hole collapsed and was covered up by the top soil that was around it, with the giant pink pearl bouncing off and landing next to Kimo's feet!

"We've got to hurry, Kimo. I need to get back to OI86 and see if I can help Sophie and Scottie."

As Professor Zooger's divers were trying to get out of the air chamber, Sophie and Scottie could see that the room was beginning to fill up with ocean water. Otto was trying to escape along with the panicked divers, but kept getting pushed out of the way. Finally, Otto was the last one in the chamber and was just about to go through the hatch and it struck—a violent earthquake that began to close the walls of the ravine onto the submarine. The eels began to scatter and swam back to their rock crevices near the coral cavern. The air chamber wasn't quite covered, so the girls could see Otto staying above the rising ocean water, nose and paws pressing against the glass as he tried to get out.

"Quick, Sophie, we've got to swim over there and try to get Otto out. Maybe the earthquake put a crack into one of the glass sections that we can break open to get to him," Scottie yelled as she swam toward the chamber.

"Wait, Scottie, look out in the ocean. Something is coming and it's coming fast!"

"Oh, my gosh, I think it's a torpedo!" Scottie replied as she and Sophie were trying to stop themselves from getting closer to the chamber in the crazy current.

Just as she said that, a large dark object zoomed past the girls at ramming speed and then crashed against the chamber! It was Bubbles. She had grown twice her size and was black as night. She circled again as the glass in the chamber began to crack. At ramming speed again she headed for the chamber, even faster than a torpedo this time. SLAM! Once again, the girls could hear the impact against the chamber. The next sound was unmistakable. It reminded the girls of walking on the frozen pond at the ranch in winter when the ice would start to crack with an eerie sort of twisting and scratching sound.

"Look, Scottie. Bubbles did it!" Sophie pointed to the chamber. "The glass is cracking all over the chamber."

"Quick, look over there! I can see a large hole in the top of the glass," Scottie said. "I can see that the room is filling up with water, and Otto won't have long before he can breathe again."

The girls swam as quickly as possible and were able to get Otto out of the chamber as the water rose to the top of the broken opening of the chamber. Sophie pulled a lifeless Otto out and cradled him in her arms as both girls swam to the surface.

"Come on, Otto, you can do this...BREATHE!" Scottie shouted.

Just as she said that, another diver joined them on an aqua scooter. It was Dr. Drake! He quickly took Otto and began CPR, using his regulator. Within minutes, Otto began to cough in little sneezing type sounds and looked around as if to ask what all the fuss was about.

Bubbles swam over to them as well, now back to normal size but still a very deep purple color. She began to swim around the group and saw that Otto was going to be fine. She leaped out of the water, doing flips as if she were performing for Otto. As they all began to laugh, they could feel the hair on their arms begin to stand up.

"What's happening, Uncle Drake?" Scottie shouted as she looked around in the water and at Sophie.

"Look above you," Uncle Drake suggested.

As if the coral cavern had opened up toward the sky, the electrical currents from the eels had an effect on all of the colorful coral, sending electrical charges up the sea kelp and releasing huge colorful sparks high into the air!

"Wow!" both girls shouted.

"There must be hundreds of bursts, just like in the cavern," Sophie described.

"Yes, but much, much larger!" Scottie agreed.

As the sky seemed to calm down, Bubbles noticed an aqua scooter race past underneath them and nudged Sophie to look down. Sophie told Scottie and Uncle Drake to look into the water and all realized it was Professor Zooger and Lurch! Professor Z stopped to look up and to his horror recognized Dr. Drake and the girls. He immediately turned and put the throttle to full power in order to distance himself from not only Sophie and Scottie but also Bubbles' speed and powerful strength.

"Quick, we have to catch him," Scottie ordered.

But it was too late. The professor and Lurch got into a speed boat that was waiting for them seconds before Bubbles was about to bump them off of their scooters.

"It looks like Zooger's divers got out of the sub in time and were able to radio for help," Uncle Drake observed. "Well, Professor Z can't do any harm to the island now. His hut is destroyed and…"

"And so is his submarine!" Scottie cheered.

After she said that, Otto let out a loud squeal and began to clap while rolling around on the surface of the water, making everyone laugh.

"Okay, girls, I want you to swim back to the coral cavern so I don't have to explain to Maddie or anyone else why you don't have any diving gear on," Uncle Drake ordered with a smile. "I will meet you under the plumeria trees."

Sophie, Scottie, and Otto gave Uncle Drake a big hug and were on their way, holding on to Bubbles as she swam back to the cavern.

CHAPTER FOURTEEN

Summer Solstice

The coral cavern never looked so beautiful, the girls thought, as they stood up onto the rock platform. Bubbles was right behind them and reached for a nearby towel as she turned back into Amelia. Sophie and Scottie stepped out of the water first, with Otto scampering around their legs with excitement.

"Otto reminds me so much of Molly," Scottie said with a laugh as she reached down to pet him.

"Boy, Molly would love to play with Otto in our pond," Sophie added.

"While you two dry off, I will get dressed and then meet your uncle at the plumeria trees. I'm sure he wants to make sure you are all safe," Amelia suggested as she walked toward her dressing chamber.

Sophie and Scottie dried off and put their clothes

on over their swimsuits. As they waited for Amelia and Uncle Drake to get back, the girls walked into the treasure room.

"I'll never get used to all of this beautiful treasure that Otto has found," Scottie sighed as she surveyed all of the items.

"I know," Sophie agreed and picked up a beautiful gold and pearl bracelet. "I don't think anyone should find out about this place or the tide pools, and I'm sure Uncle Drake feels the same way."

"Yes, I do agree with you," Uncle Drake said, holding the giant pink pearl as he walked up to the girls to give them each a hug. "You two helped put into motion the demise of Professor Zooger's plan to destroy the island for his own selfish gain."

"I want to thank you two for your bravery and your ability to work together to solve the island's fishy mystery!" Amelia said enthusiastically to Sophie and Scottie as she took the pearl from Uncle Drake.

"Yes, without your teamwork, I don't think we would've ever figured out how important Amelia is to this island," Uncle Drake said. "Now, I have a suggestion that I think will ensure Amelia's safety when we are no longer here."

"What would that be?" both girls asked at the same time.

Uncle Drake looked at Amelia and said, "There is a very dedicated director of the institute that would love to meet you and work with you to preserve this island. In fact, the poster in the library of the other Amelia belongs to this person."

"Are you talking about Maddie?" Amelia asked.

"Why, yes, I am," Uncle Drake replied in an assured tone.

"I've been observing her when she eats in the cafeteria and I've always wanted to meet her. In fact, whenever she dives, I try to swim near her to see what she is studying and to make sure that she is safe," Amelia added.

"Good. I will ask her to meet us for breakfast at the ranch tomorrow morning and then Sophie, Scottie, and I will bring her to the plumeria trees. It will be up to you, Amelia, to tell her that you are also Bubbles if you want to. She has always suggested that there are forces on this island that aren't scientifically explainable. Therefore, she will be honored to learn about the coral cavern and do what is necessary to protect it."

"That would be great! Now girls, I know that Otto already gave you each a necklace, but now you can pick a piece of jewelry for your very own if you'd like to—something to remind you of this place and me," Amelia said with a smile.

"Oh, we'd never forget you, Otto, or this beautiful place!" Scottie exclaimed as she walked over to give Amelia a hug.

"You can say that again," Sophie said with a smile and became a little teary-eyed as she also walked over to hug Amelia. "Would it be okay to bring this bracelet for our mother?"

"Oh, that is a perfect choice, you bet," Amelia agreed. "And I won't ever forget you girls either. You will need to come back and visit some day."

"Alright, girls, Amelia needs to get some rest and

we need to get some dinner!" Uncle Drake announced. "We'll be back after breakfast with Maddie."

Amelia walked them back to the entrance of the lava tube and they were on their way to the ranch in the ATV.

Uncle Drake parked near the stables, so the girls could check on the horses and see if their horseshoes were okay. To their relief, Starburst and Firefly's hooves looked healthy and the horseshoes were secure.

"Let's go grab some dinner and then you girls should head to your yurt to make sure Maptrixter is okay," Uncle Drake stated as he began to walk toward the cafeteria.

"Sounds good. We're starved!" Sophie said while walking next to Scottie and Uncle Drake.

Kimo noticed the three of them coming into the cafeteria and walked up to Uncle Drake as they got their food.

"I don't really know what was going on out past the ranch with the fireworks, that crazy hut, and the earthquake, but is everything secure now on the island?" Kimo asked.

"It is now. That man with the patch you may have seen getting supplies now and then on the island was a real troublemaker named Professor Zooger. He was encouraged to leave this area by Sophie and Scottie and some interesting ocean, uh, friends," Dr. Drake answered with a little snicker of a laugh.

"I see. Well, I'm glad to hear that all is under control and if that Zooger fellow comes here again, we will be ready for him," Kimo stated in a determined tone.

"I'm sure you will be ready," Dr. Drake replied and slapped him on the back with appreciation. He then looked at Sophie and Scottie and said, "Since we're finished with dinner, I think it's time we get cleaned up and got some sleep."

As they walked back to their yurts, Scottie noticed a soft glow coming from under their door and began to walk faster.

"I'll come by in the morning to get you two for breakfast. I think we'll ride over to the plumeria trees in the morning, and I'll let Maddie know this as well."

"Okay, Uncle Drake, we'll see you tomorrow," Sophie agreed as they walked into their yurt.

When the girls walked into the room, everything seemed normal except for one thing. The top dresser drawer was glowing and trying to open!

"I think we'd better check that drawer," Scottie said while unzipping her backpack.

As Sophie opened the drawer, Maptrixter leaped out and landed on the lower bunk bed. Then her rain box hopped out of the drawer and landed on the table next to where Scottie was standing! After the rain box landed, its lid popped off and the frame inside of the box began to glow.

"I'd better take the frame out of the rain box," Sophie suggested.

As soon as she did this, the frame began to change into multiple colors of orange, yellow, green, blue, purple, and red. And then it began to grow to the size of a television that would be in someone's home. After it was done growing, the girls had to rub their eyes because they could see words being written onto the area of the frame where a picture would go! It read:

Dear Sophie and Scottie,
Great job in solving the fishy mystery! I knew you could do it, but you are needed back at the ranch. It looks like there is a storm brewing and you are needed to help your father secure the animals. Please do the following after breakfast in the morning: Ride Starburst and Firefly to the edge of the cliffs where the trail on Maptrixter is glowing. As you get to the end of the trail, Sophie, give Scottie the frame from your backpack. Put this frame on the trail with the front of it facing you both at 9:55 in the morning. As you get back onto Starburst, Scottie, ride as far back on the trail as possible with Sophie on Firefly just behind you. Then you will see what happens next!
Love,
Auntie Jill

"I guess our adventure is coming to an end," Sophie commented and then suddenly the frame shrunk back to a smaller size. The message faded away and Sophie put the frame into her backpack next to the rain box.

"Yes, and according to that mysterious letter, I get to put the frame on the trail again," Scottie added. "And look, the trail is glowing on Maptrixter, near the plumeria grove."

184

"We'd better pack up and be ready to go when Uncle Drake comes by in the morning," Sophie directed as she began to pull her backpack onto her bed to put her clothes in it. She rolled up Maptrixter and made sure it was in the main part of her pack with the rain box and the frame carefully put in her outer pocket.

Morning seemed to come quickly and the girls were looking forward to seeing Maddie at breakfast.

"Good morning, girls. Happy summer solstice!" Uncle Drake stated as he opened up the door to their yurt, with Papaya on his shoulder letting out a squawk that made everyone laugh.

"What is summer solstice?" Scottie asked as she grabbed her backpack and looked around the yurt for one last time.

"Oh, sis, it's the first day of summer. Everyone knows that," Sophie said in a teaching tone as she put her backpack on.

"Well, NOW everyone knows," Scottie replied and put on her pack to follow them to breakfast.

"Good morning, Sophie, Scottie, and Dr. Drake," Maddie greeted as she waited for them to reach her.

"Good morning, Miss McKenzie," both girls replied.

"Let's grab some food, and then we'll map out to-day's events," Dr. Drake suggested as they got in line in the cafeteria.

Once everyone was settled at the table, Dr. Drake began to explain where they would be going on their horse ride.

"Do you remember stating how forces on this island aren't scientifically explained?" he asked Maddie.

"Why, yes I do," Maddie answered, nodding her head.

"Good," Sophie interrupted, "because we have something to show you that..."

"That is for your eyes only!" Scottie finished.

"Hmm, I'm very curious now," Maddie enthusiastically replied. "I'm ready when you are."

Soon all were on horseback. Scottie and Sophie had made sure that Starburst and Firefly's shoes were secured to their hooves, knowing that they would be riding on another trail after leaving Maddie and Uncle Drake with Amelia. As they got closer to the plumeria trees, Papaya swooped down and landed on Uncle Drake's shoulder with a squawk as if to say "wait for me!" Sophie began to feel a little nervous and Scottie felt this way as well because they weren't sure how Maddie would react when she saw Amelia. As they rode to the end of the trail, Scottie noticed Amelia first. She was hiding behind one of the trees and put up her finger next to her mouth to make a quiet "SHH" sound. Scottie understood that Amelia didn't want to spook Maddie and didn't say anything...yet!

"Well, here we are," Sophie said while getting off Firefly.

"These trees are beautiful," Maddie admired as she looked around after getting off of her horse.

After all had dismounted, Uncle Drake walked the horses to several trees to tie their reins to the plumeria branches.

"Okay, now we just need to wait," Uncle Drake said to Maddie and the girls.

It was a beautiful day on the island for the first day of summer and the trees were as fragrant as ever.

Scottie noticed a shadow behind Maddie and held her breath in such a way that it made everyone turn toward where she was looking.

"Well, look who is here," Uncle Drake said as he gave Amelia a hug and so did the girls.

Maddie just looked at her in a shocked stare, not knowing what to do or say.

"Maddie, this is…"

"Amelia Earhart?" Maddie interrupted.

"Well, no, just Amelia," Amelia replied as she gently took Maddie's hand and shook it.

Maddie blinked a couple of times and then seemed to wake up and shake Amelia's hand as well.

"This is amazing. If I didn't know better, I'd say you were her, in the flesh, which is impossible, of course! Oh, I'm just rambling on here. It is very nice to meet you," Maddie stated nervously.

"It is very nice to finally meet you too. I've been watching you through the glass every morning when you eat breakfast. I would tell Otto when I got back to the cavern that I would love to meet you someday!" Amelia replied while still shaking her hand.

"I'm confused," Maddie began. "What do you mean by watching me through the glass with Otto, and what or where is this cavern?"

"We knew you'd have lots of questions, so I think the best way to explain everything is to show you," Dr. Drake suggested as he took each woman's arm in his and proceeded to walk into the opened lava tube, leaving Sophie and Scottie to follow… or stay behind.

"Psst, Scottie, this is the perfect time to get back on our horses and follow Auntie Jill's instructions," Sophie whispered.

Sadly, Scottie knew that this was the right time to get going, and they quietly got back on their horses as the enormous boulder slid to a grinding close.

"I would've liked to formally say goodbye to Otto and Amelia, but I know that this way is best. Now Maddie can carry on with protecting the coral cavern, Bubbles, Otto, and the island," Sophie said with a sigh as they reached the trail and headed for the cliffs near the plumeria trees.

Starburst was feeling energized and seemed to anticipate the adventure that was about to happen. Soon the girls were riding out of the plumeria trees and were looking for another trail that would lead to the island cliffs.

"Boy, Starburst sure is spirited and full of energy this morning," Sophie observed as Starburst was prancing instead of walking and was tossing her head up and down. She did this to get Scottie to loosen the reins, which signaled that it was time to gallop.

"Easy, girl," Scottie said softly and petted the side of her neck. "We're not ready to run yet."

"I think this is the trail we're supposed to go on," Sophie suggested, pointing to the trail and turning Firefly onto it.

The horses walked on the trail, getting closer to the cliffs with every step. Sophie felt something in her backpack and noticed the frame was moving around in her outer pocket. In fact, it was moving back and forth, back and forth, faster and faster! It was beginning to get hard for Sophie to sit on Firefly without almost slipping out of the saddle.

"I think this is where we should stop," Sophie ordered.

"How do you know?"

"Because the frame is sliding back and forth so much that I think it wants us to stop."

Scottie dismounted from Starburst as Sophie turned her pack around to unzip her outer pocket. Just as she did this, the frame leaped out of her pack and flew toward Scottie! Scottie almost dropped the frame as she was trying to hold onto the reins and catch the frame at the same time.

"I guess you are right, sis," Scottie said with a giggle as she handed Starburst's reins to Sophie and began to walk toward the cliff. She hadn't really looked at her wrist watch in a while and saw that it was 9:45 a.m., almost time for what, she wasn't sure. Scottie set the frame down onto the trail as Auntie Jill instructed and noticed an unusual rock formation just off the shoreline, maybe 200 feet into the water.

"Hey, look, Sophie, that rock formation looks like a mini Sleeping Giant Mountain, except it has some kind of hole through the top of it."

"Yeah, I know. I was looking at it while you set the frame down. Oh, my gosh, Scottie, you'd better hurry. It's almost 9:55!"

Scottie took Starburst's reins and held on to the horn of the saddle as she put her foot in the left stirrup and pulled herself up. Feeling rather proud of herself for not needing a rock to help her get up on her horse, she didn't notice what was happening right in front of her.

"Scottie," Sophie yelled, "look up and hold on to Starburst's reins tightly so she doesn't gallop too soon."

Scottie and Sophie noticed the frame beginning to hop up and down about two inches. Then, it happened. The sun's ray somehow found the hole in the rock formation out in the ocean water. At the perfect time, the ray pierced through the hole, reflecting on the water, and then the ray hit the frame that was on the trail. Instantly, the frame began to spark and turn multiple colors of red, green, orange, yellow, blue, and purple! As if on command, the frame grew so big that the girls couldn't see around it. Sophie looked at the frame and could see the trail on their ranch that they'd originally been on to ride to the island. But wait, something was moving in the distance. It was Molly and she was running right toward them.

"Hurry, Sophie, we've got to move now before Molly gets to us first!" Scottie shouted.

Starburst was ready to run. Her back legs were prancing back and forth as if she were in a barrel racing contest and she was about to run into the arena.

Scottie let the reins loosen and yelled "hayah!" as loud as possible.

This spooked Firefly, who began to jump forward to catch up with Starburst. It was all the girls could do to steady themselves with their backpacks on while sitting on their horses and riding back through the frame. Just as the horses' hooves touched the Shear Heaven Ranch trail, Molly was right in front of them and dodged to their right before the horses trampled her! A vacuum-packed sort of sound occurred behind the riders as the frame instantly shrunk before Sophie or Scottie could look back to see the island one last time.

"Wow, that was close!" Scottie shouted with excitement.

"Whew, we're home!" Sophie exclaimed in a relieved tone as she noticed that the frame hopped back into the outer pocket of her backpack.

Molly was now running all around the horses, jumping up and down and barking at the same time.

"Do you think she knows that we were gone from the ranch?" Scottie asked.

"I'm not sure, but it does seem like she knows something was up with our horseback, uh, ride today," Sophie answered, leaning over to try to pet Molly's head as she jumped up.

"I don't know about you, but I'm ready to head for home. It looks like it's getting a little windy out here and those are some pretty dark clouds in the distance," Scottie said while looking up at the sky.

As they headed on a trail that led to the main house, the girls could see a structure in one of the giant oak trees with Pa standing in it!

"Pa!" the girls shouted at the same time.

"Oh, I see you're back from your ride and just in time. Look what I built for you girls," Pa showed them with a beaming smile. "It's supposed to be a surprise."

"Oh, goodness," Sophie exclaimed, "it's a tree house!"

It had wooden stairs leading up to the first floor of the structure with four sides to it so no one would fall out. One of the sides was made of a lattice pattern similar to the yurt walls on the island. This pattern made it possible for the girls to see out of the tree house even if they were sitting down. Another side of the wall had a large hole in it to allow one of the tree limbs jutting out from the tree house to continue to grow. The second floor was a little smaller and also had wooden stairs leading up to it. Pa even made an A-frame roof over it to shade the "house" from the hot sun.

"We love it!" Scottie announced excitedly.

"I was hoping you two would, but we'd better get back to the house and check with the weather stations. It looks like there might be a storm coming."

Both girls wanted to get off their horses and hug Pa, but knew that it would be best to do as he said.

"Hey, what's that in your back pocket, Pa?" Scottie asked, noticing something that was rolled up and stuffed into it.

"What's that?" Pa instinctively reached back to touch his back pocket. "Oh, I forgot to take it out of my pocket at the house after I got the mail. It's an envelope from Auntie Jill for you two girls."

Sophie and Scottie turned to look at each other while sitting on their horses and knowingly mouthed to one another with wide eyes: a photograph!

To Be Continued……..

ABOUT THE AUTHOR

Cindy C. Murray

Cindy C. Murray loves sharing engaging and imaginative stories with young readers. Her creative storytelling is inspired by her two daughters and by the childhood adventures she shared with her six siblings. She has received a Bachelor of Science degree in Business Administration as well as several book awards; Silver Mom's Choice Award, Gold Family Choice Award, and Silver International Readers' Favorite. She lives in Rowlett, Texas, with her husband, visiting daughters, and two dogs.

www.cindycmurray.com

The following award winning books - Gold Family Choice Award and Silver Mom's Choice Award - by Cindy C. Murray are also available in *The Adventures of Sophie and Scottie Series*

<u>Sophie and Scottie's Adventures of the Monarch Mystery</u> - Book 1 in the series

<u>Sophie and Scottie's Adventures of Sweet Tooth Rock</u> - Book 3 in the series

Sophie and Scottie's Adventures of Sweet Tooth Rock

Sophie and Scottie were happy when they returned from Amelia Island to Shear Heaven Ranch on horseback. The magical crystal frame had shown them an amazing adventure they'd never forget. As the sisters rode closer to their ranch home, they noticed Pa in a tree house they hadn't seen before!

"Pa, you built us a tree house?" Sophie asked with delight.

"Oh, it was supposed to be a surprise," Pa answered with a smile.

"We love it!" both girls exclaimed.

"There's something in your back pocket," Scottie noticed.

"What's that? Oh, another surprise. It's an envelope from your Auntie Jill. I'll give it to you after you put the horses in their stalls because it looks like a storm is coming."

As the sisters rode to the stables, they shouted with excitement to each other, "Maybe it's a photograph!"

The storm passed and the morning sun was now shining down on the old stone house the family had stayed in over the blustery night. As Scottie looked out the window, she saw a boy helping ranch-hand Jack and Pa clean up after the storm. Who was he? Ma found the envelope and put it next to Sophie's backpack, which had the magical frame in the outer pocket. The envelope's being so close made the frame move and escape by bouncing out of her pack! Their dog, Molly, was sure to bark. How were the girls going to hide the bouncing frame with its crystals changing into a swirl of vibrant colors from Ma? With all this commotion, when would they open the envelope and notice the photo of a mountain with a peculiar rock jutting out from it and a colossal castle that was waiting for their arrival?

Find out the answers to these questions and more when you join the girls for their next magical journey in

Sophie and Scottie's Adventures of Sweet Tooth Rock!